Gerald Poole and the Pirates

by Johannes T. Evans

Gerald Poole, a young Englishman, is miserable when he is dispatched abroad aboard a naval vessel, and is reluctantly attended to by the cold and put-upon Lieutenant Jack Wicks - this tense relationship is interrupted and put under pressure when the two are kidnapped by pirates.

A novella with a little bit of adventure, romance, and queerness in the 18th century Mediterranean!

CONTENT THEMES & WARNINGS (POTENTIAL SPOILERS):

This story is set at sea in the late 18th century, and throughout there is language and behaviour typical to the period, including racism, homophobia, and ableism throughout, as well as blood and violence. It's a kidnapping narrative, and therefore consent could be considered coerced, although everybody is enthusiastically consenting.

Although there is no label applied due to the period, two protagonists are depicted as ADHD, Gerald Poole and Orion Thwaites.

Gerald Poole and the Pirates is a work of fiction created from the author's imagination. Any resemblance to living persons, living or dead, or resemblance to actual events, places, or names is purely coincidental.

Cover design by Johannes T. Evans. Art used is from Heritage Type's collation of public domain vintage art, in this case, their Nautical Nation #02 set.

Part I

"… and this is Second Lieutenant John William Wicks," said Captain Lewisham.

The captain himself was a tall man, grizzled in the way some men old beyond their years were, with hollows showing on his thickly stubbled cheeks and dark shadows underneath his eyes. His lips were darker in colour than his skin, which was naturally pale but made uncomfortably red by the sun, and he didn't look after them, it was plain to see, because they were chapped and Gerald could see a bitten mark on his lower lip.

He couldn't have been older than forty-five, but he might have passed for sixty.

Wicks couldn't have been more different.

He was the same height as Lewisham, the both of them six feet tall, but where Lewisham was thin and underfed and wiry in the way of a fox that strayed into the city, Wicks was packed with brawn and fat. His great chest was barrel-shaped, his shoulders broad, his thighs and his upper arms heavy and tough as ham hocks, and his perfectly pressed and starched uniform strained at the seams in the most wonderful of ways.

His face, Gerald was pleased to note, was quite handsome as well – he had a large head to accompany his large body, and it was a very nice head, Gerald thought, one of the finest he had seen in some time. Wicks had a strong jaw and a cleft chin, handsome, dark brown skin, thick, black hair pomaded into submission, a broad, square nose made of supremely sensible angles, and plump lips almost entirely lacking in definition, making them seem all the more kissable.

Unfortunately, Lieutenant Wicks did not give the impression of a man who wanted to be kissed – in fact, he was looking down at Gerald so coldly that he couldn't help but feel another k-word was closer to the surface of his mind.

"Hullo," said Gerald, with forced brightness. "What a beautifully starched uniform, Lieutenant."

"You were expecting a sailor in improper dress, sir?" asked Wicks without hesitation.

Gerald faltered at the briskness in his tone, and looked askance at Lewisham, whose chapped lips shifted into a small, unpleasant smile.

"Wicks will look after you in your time here, Mr Poole," said Lewisham. Gerald was distinctly aware of the double meanings present in a phrase like *to look after*. "Have you sailed before?"

"No, Captain Lewisham, I never have," said Gerald uncertainly. "But I'm sure I'll, ah, rally to meet the challenge."

"Well, Wicks' mother was in service," said Lewisham, with a sort of sneer to his voice that Gerald didn't much like the sound of, and he didn't like the way it made Wicks' face tighten either, his plump lips pursing. "I'm sure he'll be able to perform the duties you'll need of him."

"Oh," said Gerald. "Oh, Captain, I hardly need, ah, a valet—"

"For your safety, Mr Poole," said Lewisham. "I wouldn't put a young man like you, used to such…" Lewisham cleared his throat. "*Comfortable* environs among my men without a buffer. Wicks is that buffer."

Gerald didn't know what to say to that, but behind them, everyone was going down gangplanks and whatever else, and it seemed it was time to go aboard. The gangplank, as he walked down it, *moved*, the ship swaying and making the whole of the strangely slatted board move and shift under his feet.

He froze in the middle of the plank, trembling so hard he couldn't bear to so much as move his feet, but too frightened to go back. He was terrified of falling into the water – he could swim, but he didn't like the look of the deep port waters, with ships and chains and ropes all over.

Wicks came up behind him, and although his weight – he must be heavy, Gerald thought, with all that *muscle*, muscle was heavy, wasn't it? – didn't make the plank go entirely still, it did stabilise it somewhat.

"Move," said Wicks, and when Gerald kept shaking, Wicks pushed him in the lower back.

Gerald whimpered, but he didn't fall as he stumbled hurriedly forward, Wicks stepping slowly behind him up the plank, and Gerald for a moment was relieved when he fell in a pile of limbs onto the deck. He swiftly realised he was wrong about this. It wasn't quite so bad as the plank itself, because he wasn't about to be tipped into the water, but sitting on his arse on the wooden boards he could feel the whole ship moving underneath him, and it made him feel sick to his very stomach, to his very core. The nausea roiled within him.

He had travelled long periods by coach before, and sometimes he did feel a little unwell on very rough journeys, but it wasn't anything like this.

"You look pale," said Wicks as he dragged Gerald up to his feet with a hand under his elbow, and on his feet, the nausea did not immediately go away. His knees felt weak, his whole body felt weak, and he opened his mouth, but didn't manage to talk right away.

He gagged without meaning to, and Wicks propelled him abruptly to the rail so that when he vomited, it went over the side. Wicks had him lifted almost by the hips, so that the spatter didn't actually hit the side of the hull, but dropped into the water.

As Gerald watched, coughing, a few fish bobbed to the surface and started going through the mess.

"I'm so sorry," Gerald said miserably. "I've never been on a boat before, Lieutenant."

"You still haven't," said Wicks, tone dark as he offered Gerald a handkerchief to wipe his mouth with, and Gerald did so obediently. "This is a ship. Come, they've had quarters put aside for you."

"How long will it take for me to stop feeling ill?" asked Gerald.

Wicks released a derisive noise.

It was not a comforting answer.

* * *

He had very much wanted to enjoy sailing. It struck him as delightfully and incredibly exciting, to be swashbuckling upon the roiling seas, working hard under the heat from the sun, singing along with chants, and whatnot.

There was less romance in the matter when one spent a lot of one's time lying on one's side in the cupboard that had been set aside as one's quarters, feeling constantly sick and dizzy.

After a week or so at sea, he was able to becalm his stomach when the seas themselves were particularly still and they weren't moving too quickly over the waters, and he managed to read a little of his books, walk back and forth a little.

Whenever he tried to leave his little cabin for something other than mealtimes, though, Wicks would appear at his shoulder, would materialise as if from the air itself – for being such a big man, he had an extremely light step, and he moved as quickly as a shadow, when it suited him.

When it suited him, it seemed, was whenever it seemed as though Gerald might look as though he were about to go above decks, or when he tried to have a look at what any of the sailors were doing, but they all did such interesting things. Everyone was always working at something, fixing rope, repairing sails, oiling things or waxing things or nailing things together or doing joinery or whatever else, and in the mess sailors were often sleeping in their hammocks or on thin bedrolls laid out at the edge of the cramped room, or eating or drinking, or playing cards, or even reading books, which surprised him, because Gerald hadn't realised so many sailors could read.

He didn't know that all of them did, no, because some sailors would be reading aloud to others or crowding around the same little pile of pages, but more of them than he had expected could read.

Gerald had almost thought only the officers would.

Wicks didn't like it when Gerald bothered the sailors, interrupting their leisure time or speaking to them while they were working. He didn't like it when Gerald went above decks. In truth, Gerald wasn't sure he liked it when he left his cabin – and for that matter, it struck him that Wicks might prefer it were he asleep the whole time.

Just a few minutes ago, Gerald had seen one of the particularly handsome sailors with a black bruise blooming over his eye, and as soon as he'd gone to ask him about it, Wicks had burst from the ether to usher him back to his cabin and get him dressed.

"I am sorry," said Gerald as Wicks helped him into his dinner jacket. He'd been eating with the officers every evening, a guest of honour as they shipped him eastward, no matter that he didn't think they actually liked him very much – Lewisham certainly didn't seem to particularly care for him, and nor did his quartermaster, a man named Boggs. They *were* polite, never said anything untoward, but sometimes when Gerald began to chatter about something, asked questions, he'd be met with such gripping silence that it cut him to the very core.

He so hated to be met with silence, no matter what it was he'd said.

"Sorry, sir?" asked Wicks.

"That you have to keep bothering yourself with me, I mean," said Gerald. "I'm sure there are, ah, far more important ways you might be spending your time."

Wicks didn't reply.

He employed silence rather a lot.

It wasn't as though Gerald made himself, he didn't think, painfully obvious or unkind or unpleasant. He was just overwhelming, he knew, and too loud, and rather too much, as he always had been. He'd been trying to withhold himself, at least in Wicks' presence, but it made no difference, as it never did.

* * *

It was several more weeks later that Gerald was shaken awake in the dead of night with Wicks leaning over him, dragging him out of his bedclothes. It was a surprise, but no less flattering, and he laughed softly as he pulled himself to sit up in the dim light.

Wicks was unsmiling as ever, his face lit strangely by the candle light.

"Put this on," he growled.

"If that does it for you," said Gerald, feeling his cheeks burn with a pink blush, and let Wicks dress him in what appeared to be a uniform. The shirt was a little too big for him, but the jacket fit him perfectly, and Gerald couldn't help but wonder who he'd pilfered it from, because barely any of the sailors he'd seen were as petite and slim as he was, but for some of the midshipmen—

The door slammed as it was thrown open, and Gerald froze, his fingers unbuttoning Wicks' jacket as Wicks' buttoned up his.

It wasn't a face Gerald was familiar with, and Gerald looked from his face to his clothes, his open shirt and greying chest hair, his unkempt beard, his dark red trousers. Where his head of hair was black as anything on the top, his sideburns and beard were turning quick to salt and pepper, and he wore a gold hoop through one of his ears, wore a few rings, too, and tattoos covered his arms and shoulders.

He was holding a blade in his hand, its polished edge glinting in the light.

He didn't look like any sailor Gerald had seen, these past weeks, and Gerald's blood went rather abruptly cold.

The pirate in the doorway laughed at the both of them. "Get on the top deck, lads," he said. "Now's hardly the time for *that*."

Wicks kept Gerald close to him as they went above decks, and murmured, "Don't say a word."

"But—"

"*Not a word*," Wicks ordered crisply, and Gerald let his jaw click shut as they went onto the top deck. Many of the sailors were sitting in rows, cross-legged or kneeling with their heads bowed, and Gerald looked to the other ship bound close to theirs, a great many lines strung between the two of them.

Pirates were walking between the rows of people, big swords in their hands, and Gerald saw many of them held pistols too. Wicks pushed Gerald down to sit directly in front of him, and when Gerald craned his head to get a glimpse of Lewisham and who he assumed was the pirate captain, a man in a purple jacket, Wicks grabbed him by the back of his head and shoved it forward so he'd look at the floor.

Lewisham was bleeding, slouched in a chair and leaning to one side, and the ship's surgeon was holding a wet cloth to the side of his head. As Gerald looked out of the corner of his eye, fighting the desperate desire to lift his head and see properly, the pirate captain came forward.

"Hardly any reason to panic," he was advising. He was quite possibly one of the most beautiful men that Gerald had ever seen, and Gerald was arrested at the mere sight of him, his lips parted, his eyes wide.

Under the beating Mediterranean sun, the pirate captain's bronze-brown skin shone almost gold, and his brown eyes glittered like so much molten honey; his hair, which was black and tremendously fine, shimmered in the light as though the tresses themselves were woven from water, and at the places where his clothes showed the skin underneath – where his calves showed, his forearms, where his chest and neck were bared by the plunge of his loose-worn blouse – he was covered over and around with scars and tattoos. Rather like Lewisham, he wore a few rings on his fingers, but where Lewisham's rings had a sort of plain and tired quality to them, worn for his station, the pirate captain's fingers glittered with jewels and different colours in the bands of shined metal.

"We don't want to do any of you any harm," he said smoothly to the men all on their knees, walking with a cat-like grace upon the ship's boards and moving with the sway of the deck beneath him, as though the swell of the water was as natural to him as the rhythm of his own breaths, "except, of course, to your coffers." He laughed, and it was a merry, beautiful sound – he spoke with an Englishman's cadence, and Gerald was not tremendous with accents, but he struck Gerald as a merchant's son, perhaps. He was educated, but he lacked the stuffiness Gerald knew rang out in his own voice and that of his brothers – he had gone to school, but not the likes of Eton, or any school like that.

The grizzled sailor in the red trousers who'd met them downstairs moved forward, and the captain turned to greet him. The captain was taller even than Wicks, tall and graceful in the way a statue was, so much so that it almost seemed a surprise that he moved so easily; the red-trousered fellow was shorter, more like Gerald's own height, and the captain had to lean so that he could murmur in his ear.

Gerald leaned forward, craning as if he might hear some word as the captain and his lieutenant both looked in their direction, but Wicks grabbed him by the back of his neck and shoved his head again down that he face the ship's deck.

He heard them laugh.

It was out of the corner of his eye that he saw the red-trousered man hold up a leatherbound book – the captain's diary – to his captain, and Gerald watched the pirate's expression change subtly. His beautifully sculpted lips pouted slightly, and his eyes, which were heavily lidded and had thick, dark lashes, narrowed.

"Now, Captain... *Lewisham*, is it?" he asked, turning back to the captain slumped in his chair. "It seems we've been dishonest with each other. I so hate to begin a relationship on such poor terms."

Wicks' grip tightened on the back of Gerald's neck, balling up the back of his shirt, as the pirate captain stepped slowly closer to Lewisham.

"Point him out to us, won't you?" asked the pirate captain sweetly. "We'll hardly harm a hair on his head."

For a moment, Gerald thought that Lewisham was holding his tongue intentionally, but he was slumped very badly in his seat, and Gerald watched the pirate captain reach out, pulling his head up slightly by the hair. He frowned at Lewisham as the surgeon said, "Wait, wait, he's—"

"Concussed, yes, I see," said the captain distastefully. "Mr Cotton, would you?"

Gerald winced at the deafening bang when the pistol shot rang out, and Wicks dragged Gerald closer to him, shifting so that Wicks was between Gerald and the pirates on the main deck, and Gerald couldn't help the way his hands were trembling.

Captain Lewisham's body was thrown to one side, and the pirate captain and his mate, Cotton, began to make conversation with the quartermaster Boggs instead.

"We only want to ransom him," the pirate captain was saying. "Don't make us conduct a census of your crew, dear man – if you force us to do so, you will find it is writ in blood."

"I must step up," he whispered to Wicks, who shushed him. "But, Lieutenant, he just said, they'll kill another—"

Wicks elbowed him so hard in the stomach that he wheezed, unable to speak, and put his finger most demonstratively to his lips. Gerald set his jaw as he tried to catch his breath.

The captain and Cotton both had their pistols in hand as they began to make their way up and down the rows of kneeling sailors, occasionally nudging one of them to raise their heads with the muzzle of their guns or the very tip of their blades. The other pirates were hard at work, either guarding the sailors and keeping them in place, or hauling their plunder from the Ambition onto their own vessel.

They were an efficient lot, and they moved fast.

At some point, the captain and his second shared a few words and began walking the rows again, encouraging every sailor to show the palms of his hands, and Gerald didn't understand this until Cotton stood before him and prompted him to show his.

Gerald was about to when Wicks got to his feet and bore down on the smaller man, shoving him back. Knelt on the floor, Gerald let out a horrified noise as multiple pistols were aimed at Wicks, but he didn't flinch or move away from his place, keeping his gaze on Cotton.

"I'll thank you to keep your hands off my boy," said Wicks.

Cotton raised his salt-and-pepper eyebrows. "*Your* boy?" he repeated, looking between Gerald and Wicks. He stepped forward to grab for Gerald again, but Wicks grabbed him by the throat, and Gerald stared at the way Cotton's eyes went wide, scrambling wildly for purchase as Wicks lifted him up on his toes. Cotton lost his grip on his weapon and sent it clattering to the ground, and without thinking Gerald whipped it up and stood to his feet at Wicks' side, although he was trembling so much that the blade shook like a rudder.

The pirate captain was moving very slowly and carefully, one hand raised – he was telling his crew, however silently, not to shoot at Wicks and Gerald, not whilst Wicks had their own Mr Cotton suspended by his neck, coughing and spluttering.

"You're terribly bold," said the pirate captain softly. He wasn't *quite* as tall as Wicks after all, perhaps an inch or two shorter than him, but no matter his height up close, he remained quite the imposing figure.

"I don't like for men to touch my valet," said Wicks.

"Your "valet", is he?" asked the pirate captain as he leaned closer, the better to examine Gerald, and Gerald did his best to keep his chin raised, his grip tight on the trembling weapon in his fist, though it was heavier than he'd expected, and his arm already felt tired. "Were you above asking one of the shavers to relieve you?"

Lieutenant Wicks didn't say a thing, his lips twisting into a scowl, and the captain laughed at both of them – at Gerald particularly, Gerald thought, because Gerald's cheeks were burning with a hot blush, and he couldn't make them stop.

"Of course, navy men really aren't meant to bugger one another," said the captain, directing his words to Gerald instead of to Wicks. "But there are always special rules for the rich aboard, hm? You, valet. Come here."

Gerald took a hesitant step forward, but with the hand not holding Cotton on his toes, Wicks reached out and hauled him back, once more by the back of his shirt. It was Gerald's turn, this time, to drop the sword, and as soon as it hit the deck the captain caught it with the toe of his boot and dragged it behind him.

"Come now," he said smoothly, spreading his hands, but Gerald's head was whirling with how fast he'd moved, "I'd hardly harm the *servant* of such a profitable hostage, Gerald. I am correct, I suppose, in calling you Gerald?"

"You may call me Poole, if it suits you," said Wicks, and Gerald bit his tongue to keep from protesting. For all the uncommon and unpleasant circumstances, it was the first time Gerald had heard his name from Wicks' mouth, and he found he rather liked the way it sounded there, even though Wicks was clipping in his accent somewhat to be more like Gerald's.

"Gerald," purred the captain, "do unhand my quartermaster, or I shall do more than lay hands on your valet – would it upset you more were I to kill him, or if I had some like-minded members of my crew have him in front of you?"

Quartermaster Cotton's heels hit the deck, and he gasped in a wheezing breath.

"Yes," said the captain, straightening and tapping his own chin as Cotton stumbled back to his elbow. "I thought that might do the trick. Where is it you're going to?"

"Rome," said Wicks, not loosening his grip on Gerald's shirt. "We're to make berth at Fuimicino."

"Family there?" asked the captain. "With a great deal of money, one presumes, given what you're travelling with – have they money that they might like to pay to have you back? Or are you a bastard?"

"I carry the same name as that which is on your merchant's shipment, don't I?" asked Wicks coolly.

"Is that what makes legitimacy in these strange times?" was the prompt reply. "A name?"

"He *is* a bastard," growled Cotton, and the captain sympathetically patted his arm as he coughed.

"I'll go with you if you'll do no more harm," said Wicks.

"Harm? Me? Pish posh, nothing could be further from my mind," said the captain.

"I'll go with you," said the lieutenant again. "So long as you don't harm anybody else, I'll be your hostage quite willingly."

"Glad to hear it. Such a *shame* blood has been spilled on your behalf already," said the captain, and Gerald felt sick, glancing back to the corpse of Captain Lewisham sprawled on the floor, blood pooling underneath him. "Your papers?"

"In my cabin," said Wicks. "Let me fetch them—"

"I think your valet can do that." The captain was smiling directly at Gerald with a cool, venomous smile, and it was very beautiful indeed – it was quite a terrifying beauty, filled with intention, and Gerald stumbled back until his shoulders hit Wicks' chest. "Oh, how sweet. What's your name, valet?"

He couldn't just take Wicks' name, could he? No, that was a lieutenant's name – and it would be on the ship's register. "Justin," he blurted out.

"Justin," repeated the captain, and crooked his finger in a summoning motion.

Gerald looked back up to Wicks before he obeyed, and Wicks, looking very displeased with the situation, gave a tiny inclination of his head, so that Gerald slowly made his way forward.

When Gerald stood before the captain, he stroked Gerald's cheek, and Gerald shivered because his hands were cold, but it was plain that he wasn't doing this for Gerald's benefit – the whole while he was touching him, he was watching Wicks, and Gerald watched Wicks' scowl deepen, his lip curling.

For the first time, Gerald realised that Wicks wasn't entirely dressed – he was wearing a jacket that wasn't his own, stripped of bands and epaulettes so that he showed no rank, and before Gerald could focus on this too terribly, the captain took hold of Gerald's own partly unbuttoned blouse and began to finish the job that Wicks hadn't finished earlier.

“Does your master treat you very well, Justin?” asked the captain softly.

Gerald nodded.

“And do you warm his bed very obediently?”

Gerald looked away, cheeks burning, and the captain chuckled.

"Such a shy thing. Hardly meant for life at sea, but one presumes you have other attractive features," the captain said, forcing Gerald's chin up to look at him, and Gerald swallowed hard. "Collect your master's papers," he ordered in neat, crisp tones, and Gerald nodded rapidly.

One of the other pirates went below decks with him as he quickly fetched his papers, and Gerald’s mind was running fast as he dug them out of his chest, mind ticking over and over, even as the pirate picked up his valuables – his fine pocket watch that he never wore because it was too heavy, his cash, some nice cufflinks he hated to wear because of how they caught on things. He couldn’t possibly allow Wicks to do this, but if he stopped him now, surely he might cause more harm – what if they killed Wicks for having deceived them, or killed more of the crew?

But if they did take Wicks, he would have to pay the ransom himself, he simply *would have to*, for he couldn’t bear to have poor Wicks die for his sake when he’d already caused him so much trouble, and—

Gerald cried out at the hard hand in his hair, shoving him against the railing as his papers were snatched free, and he whimpered at the tight grip the pirate quartermaster had on him.

“Oh, do stop it, Mr Cotton,” said the pirate captain chidingly. “We want our guest to see we bear him no ill will, don’t we?”

Gerald was shivering as Cotton’s hand, which was heavy and calloused, slipped down to the back of his neck before pulling free.

Wicks' own strong hands had been bound at the small of his back, and before Gerald could go to him, Boggs took him by the shoulder and led him to stand with their officers, away from it all.

"How do I help?" he asked, and Boggs replied, "Say nothing. Captain Lewisham and Lieutenant Wicks have each made their sacrifices for your sake – you'll do nothing by revealing them now."

"But—"

"Wicks is doing his duty. *Shht.*"

The pirates were moving fast with their inventory, tossing over the bales of silk and other stock the Pooles traded in extremely quickly, nearly finished now. The sea was getting choppier beneath them, and it made Gerald uneasy and unsteady on his feet, nausea rising in his stomach.

He saw Wicks being made to cross the gangplank between the two ships, and he bit the inside of his lip.

His Italian was quite good – as soon as they made berth at the nearest port, he would go somewhere, send word to his aunt about Wicks, beg that if she were informed he was being held hostage to go along with it. Would his family go along with it? He would hope so, they would have to, they couldn't possibly—

"Ah, please—!" he cried out as Cotton hauled him once more by the hair, but this time dragged him forward and away from the grasping hands of Boggs and the Ambition's officers, toward and then over the gangplank. The wood was wobbling underneath them and Gerald almost sobbed, terrified they'd stumble and fall into the white-washed water swirling between the vessels aside one another, and he was almost grateful when he was tossed to the deck in front of the pirate captain.

"My valet is worth nothing to you," growled Wicks, and the pirate captain laughed, stroking his fingers through Gerald's hair as though he were little more than a dog on the floor.

"He seems to be worth quite a bit to you though, sir – I think you'll forgive me for wanting a little leverage to keep you in line, hm?"

Gerald choked, scrabbling uselessly at the captain's breast as he was hauled up by surprisingly strong hands, gripped around the neck and the jaw. The captain wasn't choking him – he examined Gerald with interest, turning his head one way or the other.

"We can't harm *you*, Mr Poole – it would be quite improper," said the captain, now meeting Gerald's gaze quite directly, "but we can harm him, if we need to. A rich young man like yourself has no doubt availed of a whipping boy before."

Wicks set his jaw, and as the gangplank was pulled out, the lines between the Ambition and this new vessel cut, Gerald let out a reedy sound despite himself.

"Poor pet," said the captain, curling his cool fingers in Gerald's hair. "Not to worry – if you both behave, neither of you needs to come to any harm."

Gerald looked helplessly to Mr Wicks. Mr Wicks looked back.

When they pushed off they were sailing, Gerald thought, in another direction, away from the mainland – the pirates had cut half the ropes on the Ambition, and they'd need quite some time to rerig all their sails to keep them from hanging so flat. This ship was smaller and faster than the Ambition, even without the other not being able to make chase.

A day's head start was all they would need, and the sun was beginning to rise properly over the horizon.

Lieutenant Wicks was installed below decks in a small room near the captain's office – it was not a brig, just a small and cramped cabin that primarily seemed to store a few additional crates and barrels, but it had two beds at least.

"Ah ah," said the captain to Gerald as he made to follow Wicks inside, holding him back.

Wicks scowled, standing straight with his hands still tied behind his back, and the captain smiled at him.

"Really, Mr Poole," he said, pulling Gerald close beside him, one of his hands splayed over Gerald's hip, "you hardly need a valet now, do you?"

Gerald tried to lean away, to pull free, but the captain's hand slid up to grip him around his throat instead, and Gerald let out a sharp, choked noise as he was pulled hard against his chest. The buttons on his coat were pressing into Gerald's back, and Gerald whimpered – he could see the twist on Wicks' face as the captain kicked the door shut, and locked it.

"You see," the captain murmured in Gerald's ear as he pulled free the key and dropped it into one of his pockets, his breath hot, his teeth grazing the shell of Gerald's ear and his hand a hot grasp around the whole of his throat, "your master's life is quite invaluable. Yours is the opposite."

"I hardly see why you need us both, then," whispered Gerald.

"You've heard of insurance," said the captain. He did bite at Gerald's ear this time, nipped at the lobe in a way that made Gerald go weak at the knees for all he was meant to be steadfast, and the captain laughed at him. "And you hardly seem upset."

"Of course I'm— Of course I'm upset—"

"I know your sort, *Justin*," said the captain, and let go all at once. Gerald stumbled and almost fell to his knees, but instead he veered and leaned back against a little dresser, turning his glare on the captain as he went to look at his reflection in the mirror, adjusting the tail of his hair tied neatly at the base of his neck.

"My sort?" repeated Gerald.

"Ever taken away with men more impressive than yourself."

"You think you're more impressive than I am? What, because you—you kidnap people, and kill them, and commit acts of piracy and intimidation?"

"I hardly think it matters what I think makes me impressive, young man," said the captain primly, and gave Gerald a crescent curve of a smile. "Your cock seems convinced that I am either way."

It was too low a blow, offensive and outrageous and blunt and uncouth, and it made the blood burn hot in his veins – perhaps because of the truth in it above all else – and Gerald lunged.

This, he knew almost as soon as he moved, was a grave error.

The captain hardly even seemed angry as, in one smooth movement, he sidestepped Gerald's clumsy pounce, grabbed him by the hair, and swung him around to bend him over his desk. Gerald hadn't even a moment to move before a blade was pressed up against the small of his back where his shirt was ruched up by the position.

The blade tip was incredibly cold and painfully sharp, resting just below his last rib.

"You know," said the captain in calm, conversational tones, "were I to push just so, I expect I could pull your heart out. Skewer it, twist, and pull it free – rather as one pulls a cooked snail from its shell."

Gerald swallowed hard, too terrified to make a sound or to cry out or to even cry, and the captain chuckled.

"I become more impressive by the moment, don't I?" he asked with a sort of syrupy glee, and then pulled back the blade, sheathing it at his hip. "Do behave yourself, darling. I should hate to make a mess."

The pirate captain then did something so painfully and offensively ordinary that it made Gerald all but burst: gripping Gerald by the hips, he pushed him aside, and with that he sank down into his seat, doused his pen in a bottle of ink, and made to update his log.

Gerald stood beside him, stunned.

“What are you doing?” he demanded.

“Oh, have you not observed this practice before?” asked the captain, noting down the time and their coordinates from the charts pinned out to his left.

Gerald sank hard into a nearby stool, and the captain chuckled. The captain, it transpired, was named Orion Thwaites, as this was noted in his logs, and he wrote for some period in his diary as Gerald sat aside.

He expected, when he grew bored and stood to his feet, for Thwaites to scold him and bid him sit again, but he didn’t – Gerald walked around the narrow, cosy space of the captain’s office, which to his surprise was packed with books and glass cases mounted on the wooden walls, filled with little cards.

He must have had twenty or thirty of them, mounted like little portraits, but there was scarcely any art in them – they were trade cards for various traders and merchants, selling everything from books to iron studs to undergarments.

Gerald’s gaze fell upon one of them, a piece of parchment paper carefully etched with a printed ship in full sails, underneath it was signed: **JAS. POOLE, MERCER & SILK TRADER, Selleth of all Sorts of fine Gold & Silver Brocades, Velvets, & Rich Silks, Wrought Workt Bedhangings, Carpets & Blankets; Likewise, Linnen, Jacques and Gowns cover’d whole, with all Sorts of Linnen Furniture at the Lowest Prices.**

“You know of Mr Poole’s father, then?” asked Gerald quietly.

“More comment would be made on it were Mr Poole a Moor, I think,” said Thwaites. “And more still were it the case that his wife was.”

“You think he’d put it on his trade card?”

“I think other people would mention it. There’s nothing an Englishman likes more than to comment on another man’s appearance, and find in it some sin or fatal flaw that assures him of his superiority.”

"I suppose," said Gerald uncertainly, not knowing how to respond to that, nor even really how to digest it.

He had noticed that Wicks was the only dark-skinned face amongst the officers of the Ambition, and that even among the ordinary sailors, there were no other Africans, but Wicks' accent was a Bristolian one, and Gerald had never heard him speak a tongue other than English aboard the ship. "You have some deep fascination with advertisements?"

"I find them charming," said Thwaites.

"Charming?"

"Quite. There's something amusing about the whole of an enterprise being summarised on a piece of card paper in the hopes of attracting new business, and I like the variety in their prints and typography."

Gerald wrinkled his nose, looking at the glass casements, and then looking at the back of Thwaites' head. "What a queer thing to enjoy," he remarked.

"As you say."

Captain Thwaites did not look up from what he was writing upon, busying himself with writing on and then blotting the page, and so Gerald looked about the other shelves, at the other books. When his hand touched the knob of the door into the corridor, Thwaites did not lift his head, but he did clear his throat quite loudly.

Gerald sat obediently down again.

"Are *you* a bastard?" he asked.

"I've received reviews that use the word," said Thwaites. He was not as provoked as Gerald had distantly hoped he might be, and kept on working. "But no, my father and my mother were married. My mother hails from Madras, and returned to England with my father when he changed commissions."

“He was a sailor? In the navy?”

“Mm, he was a merchant trader, like Mr Poole’s father.”

“Don’t you think he would be ashamed of you?”

Thwaites laughed. “What a charming idea. Perhaps – I hadn’t given it much thought.”

Finding no purchase upon which to dig his heels, Gerald asked, “What happens if they don’t pay the ransom? Mr Poole’s family?”

“I suppose the two of you shall simply have to otherwise compensate us for our hospitality.”

Looking up from his paperwork, the captain smiled at Gerald in a way that made him fidget.

The sea had been getting choppier as they crossed from one vessel to the next, and as they moved quick over the surface of the water away from where the Ambition was stranded, it seemed to Gerald initially that they were barely skimming it, but soon enough the waves began to rise higher, slowing their progress.

The ship tipped and ducked in the water increasingly, and although they were maintaining a fast speed, the journey became rougher. Gerald struggled to keep his balance even sitting down, his stool moving under him, but the captain moved with the swell as he moved between his desk and his navigation table, picking his steps as easily as anything.

“Your master walks with his sea legs,” he observed when Gerald almost fell onto the floor with a sudden swell. “You have yet to grow into your own, it seems.”

Gerald glanced to the door and wondered if Wicks had his ear pressed against it.

“I’m not seasick any longer,” said Gerald. “I was at the start.”

This made Thwaites chuckle, and he leaned back to observe Gerald, his beautiful hands landing on his beautiful waist, his beautiful head tilting slightly to one side. He was tremendously well-kept – his coat was purple and had beautiful filigree, and in very good repair, and there was a heart embroidered on its breast. His moustaches and his beard were very neatly trimmed, and the hairs there had a similar healthy sheen as the long hair on his head.

"Your master enjoys to sail, and forced his poor valet to suffer along with him," he said softly. "Is that it?"

"No," said Gerald defensively, although why he felt compelled to defend Wicks' fictionalised honour – or was he defending his own? - he didn't know. "He's not like that."

"What *is* he like?"

"If you must know," said Gerald sharply, "he's not— well, you know, he's not actually taken up tremendously with manners and nobility and fanciful things, hardly wants anyone to bow and scrape to him. He just likes to have something to do, that's all."

"As good a reason as any to sodomise one's valet, I suppose."

"He doesn't!" snapped Gerald, and the captain smiled, sitting back in his handsome chair, laying his carefully manicured, tattooed hands against his chin. The tattoos, scars, and callouses on his hands were at odds with the beautiful brown sheen of his nail beds.

"Doesn't he?" asked Thwaites, in sympathetic tones. "Why, have you not asked him yet?"

Gerald crossed his arms over his chest, scowling at him, and Thwaites didn't look away.

"Why the trip to Rome, then?" he asked.

"I hardly feel it's correct to discuss Mr Poole's business with his kidnapper."

"Well, when *correct* might get you killed, wrong is the way to go, I always say," said Thwaites.

Gerald felt himself pale slightly, but the captain didn't even blink.

"His aunt wants a house looking after, further north. No one will bother him there or know his name, but for his relation to her, and he can get on with things. He wants to pick olives."

The captain peered at him in such bafflement that Gerald was surprised. "Pick olives? Why ever would he want to do that?"

Gerald, embarrassed, said, "I don't know."

"As his valet, I presume, you are expected to join in?"

"It doesn't sound so bad."

"It's tremendously hard work, picking olives," said Thwaites, "and a delicate creature like you shall burn fast in the sun. I can tell you've been below decks nearly this whole journey – you're pale as fresh cream."

"Well, I'm sure I do look pale, next to you and Mr Poole," said Gerald, and Thwaites laughed at him. "And in any case, it's different. Being on deck. There's— I'm liable to get in the way, I expect. And— and there are birds."

"Birds? There are no birds on a ship's deck."

"The quartermaster, Boggs, he has one. Had one. Parrot sort of thing."

A truly unpleasant bird it had been too – whenever he'd gone to dine with the officers, the horrible little creature would be there, and would curse at him in French, and try to bite him.

The captain laughed his hardest yet now, and said, "You mean to tell me, darling, that before we took you captive, a cockatoo was your hostage taker?"

Gerald felt himself burn red with humiliation, but he was spared anything further as there was a crisp knock upon the captain's office door, and it pushed open to reveal Mr Cotton.

"You want us to keep this speed, Captain?" he asked.

"Who's at the wheel?"

"Creed."

The captain frowned slightly. "He wants to slow down?"

"He'd like for us to go full sail," said Cotton dryly. "I know you trust him as helmsman, but he doesn't half scare everyone shitless."

Thwaites sighed. "Very well," he said, and stood.

Gerald watched him from his place sitting down, and Thwaites watched him expectantly, one of his eyebrows raising.

"I'll behave," he attempted, trying to stop himself from glancing to the door behind which Wicks was held captive.

"You certainly will," agreed Thwaites. "On your feet, and up you come with us."

Gerald stood, and with the sudden movement of the ship beneath him, abruptly fell down after: Mr Cotton half carried him up to the top deck.

* * *

Cotton had gone through his pockets and divested him of his pocket knife and watch, but there was a nail loose on one of the crates piled in the corner of the little room, and Jack was at least able to loosen the binds around his wrists to pull them free, so that he didn't have to linger with his hands behind his back.

His shoulders hurt, but not tremendously, and he rolled them out as he sat on the floor to listen at the door as Poole and the captain spoke.

In the past few weeks, he had heard Poole talk about almost everything under the sun – Poole had a habit of talking almost to fill silence, or so it seemed to Jack, and as soon as someone was in his presence he began to speak as though someone had wound him up at the back, and he couldn't stop until he was wound down again.

Jack had listened – whilst trying not to – about cloths, silks, brocades, and velvets, about weaving techniques, about how fabrics were dyed, about how they were marketed and sold and in what sort of bales; when chatter about his father's business had done little to prompt Jack's engagement, he had moved on to talking about card games and other games played in gentlemen's parlours, about sports and field games, about amusements at fetes and fairs that he had attended; he had attempted to speak on the subject of food, discussing different candies, stews, roasted meats, wines, and beers – although alcohol in significant quantities apparently made Poole very ill, which to look at him, frail and pale as he was, was no great surprise.

When not talking *about* something, he was asking questions, and Jack rarely answered these – he had made some attempts in the first instances, but had soon realised that answering one of Poole's questions was only liable to prompt five or six more in quick succession, and that not answering any questions led to fewer of them overall.

He still didn't know what to make of him.

The other men on the Ambition had made sport of talking about him, speculating as to why he was being shipped off to Italy – if he had been caught embezzling from his father's pockets, if he was being sent off for the sake of his poor health as he constantly seemed green, pale, or flushed, and often a combination of the three, if perhaps the family were sending him off in the hopes of not hearing him talk any more.

Apparently Mr Poole had gotten onto a friend in the naval service to dispatch his son with some haste on the first possible vessel going east, and Captain Lewisham had drawn the short straw – he didn't speak of it with the petty officers, of course, but Jack had heard word bandied between the surgeon and two of the midshipmen, and of course, that word had spread.

Regardless of the reason they'd been saddled with him, it only made sense that it was Jack Wicks who had to be saddled with him particularly – Captain Lewisham had been all but salivating at the opportunity to drop ninety pounds' worth of useless labour in Jack's lap, best befitting *his proper station*, as Lewisham was so pleased to call it if Jack was in earshot, and no doubt called it something far harsher when he was not.

It wouldn't have been quite so infuriating, Jack didn't think, were it not for the fact that Poole, airheaded little twit that he was, didn't seem to understand that Jack had been assigned his personal attendant as a *slight*. Oh, he apologised, he said quite constantly how terribly sorry he was for the inconvenience of Jack having to attend him, but he didn't seem to realise that a *second lieutenant*, particularly, had better things to be doing than dressing such a strange, skinny creature in his dinner clothes and sending him off for his supper, or babysitting him to keep him from wandering into the midst of the sailors who would be delighted to tear him to pieces.

They'd all have made a great sport of that, too, knowing that Jack would get the flack if Poole came to any harm, benefits all around – they'd scarcely harm him physically, of course, or at least, not hurt him very badly and not be obvious about doing it, but it was what they'd *say* that Jack didn't want to have to deal with, not if Poole made any complaint of it or even a mention of it at his sit-down dinners.

He'd lost his temper with one of them, Foyett, when he'd said something about Poole likely being a sodomite and being shipped off to Italy to keep his hands off of the staff – this might well be true, no matter that it was an unsavoury and distasteful thing to say, but when Foyett had gone on to imply that Jack was likely servicing him in this manner as well as the others, Jack had punched one of his lights out.

There'd been a bare respite, at least, in the aftermath of this, and now—

Sitting with his back against the door, his elbows rested on his knees and his mouth against his hands, he listened to Poole say, "I suppose," and at least have the good sense – or more likely, the general distracted stupidity – not to argue that Mr Poole couldn't *possibly* be a bastard.

He'd done well, not mentioning it in the course of his deception, but it hardly mattered now – if he'd managed to get aboard this pirate ship and left Poole behind on the Ambition, he might have had the barest chance at leaving Poole alive, no matter that his own chances of survival were like as not very low, but now? What was the point?

They'd lied and managed to carry a false identity forward, the both of them, and all it amounted to was wearing false faces in the same situation as they'd have been in – except that Jack wouldn't have been in it, and Poole could have fared alone.

Jack rather hated the part of himself that wished that were the case, and he exhaled, dropping his face into his hands.

It wasn't fair.

Nothing was fair, of course – his father had been cracked when he'd said that Jack might have hopes of his own commission in some decade when he'd joined up, and Jack had told him so, but he'd hoped of *something*, and he had progressed somewhat, but this...?

This would be his end.

If he got Poole out of it, at the very least, it would lend some credence to the name of John William Wicks, something that perhaps his mother and father could be proud of, and if he got out himself, what then? A promotion to *Lieutenant*?

He wondered at times if he should just resign, but it wouldn't be easier anywhere else, and he would be liable to be called a turncoat for leaving the navy – and he loved the sea. He loved sailing, loved the sea, loved the *work*, and would love it far more were it not for every other *fucking* sailor—

Outside, he heard the door close shut, and the captain's office silent.

Jack, resigned to it, dropped himself onto the lower bunk in the room, and slept.

* * *

Gerald was not better on his feet in the cold and bracing wind that greeted them when they were in the open air. He shivered and wrapped his arms around himself, stumbling in the sea spray on the slippery deck, and Thwaites surprised him by slipping his own coat off his shoulders and tossing it to him.

Gerald nearly tipped over at the sudden new weight, but he didn't argue, and wrapped the purple coat around his shoulders, huddling in it. Thwaites, being a good deal bigger than him, left a lot of space in his coat, and Gerald sighed at how warm it was.

Gerald had no sense of time, but he didn't think they were through the day yet nearly at all, yet the skies were darkening over their heads. The ship pitched from one side to the other as they cut quick through the white-chopped water, and Gerald stumbled and slipped as he did his best to follow after the captain.

The sailors on this ship were just as loud as the navymen had been, loudly calling to one another as they worked, but the captain's voice was the loudest of all: over the billow of the sails, the creak of the ropes, the roar of the wind, his voice rang clear, and Cotton's voice echoed his.

What the devil any of it meant, Gerald hadn't much idea, but he could see that the sails were drawn in somewhat, closer to the mast, and the top most sails were folded in completely as the captain took over from the helmsman, a very neat-looking gent with gold in his ears. He and Thwaites laughed together, clapping each other on the back as they traded over positions on the wheel, and as the helmsman came away, he caught Gerald as he stumbled, skidding on the deck, and guided his hand to a railing.

Using this railing to pull himself forward, Gerald dropped heavily onto a set of crates tied fast to one edge of the deck with netting, sliding his fingers through the rope to keep himself in place.

Like Wicks, the helmsman looked to be a Moor or some other African, but they didn't look very similar at all. This man was a little taller than Wicks was and gangled in comparison: he was muscular, but in a wiry way like a rabbit, and his hair was longer and knitted into thick locks. He had rather large, very dark eyes, and sunspots freckled his brow and his cheeks, disappearing then under his thick stubble.

"A ballerina," he intoned wisely in a very deep voice, leaning gracefully to the side as he spoke so that he didn't pitch as the ship did, "stands at the bar before she takes the stage."

"Do you much like the ballet?" Gerald asked weakly, and the sailor laughed at him before walking away.

Gerald gripped fast at the wooden rail as the ship slowed somewhat, although they were still sailing – he didn't know much of the weather, but the air felt thick, and the skies above were very dark and grey. He thought it would be impossible to stay still in the storm.

"Mr— Mr Cotton, is it?" he asked, teeth chattering more for fear than the cold, and the quartermaster turned to look down at him.

"Yes?"

"That, that darkness on the horizon," said Gerald, and pointed. Cotton followed his gaze, to where the skies were turning very dark indeed, and the clouds were rolling so fast they seemed almost like unholy wheels.

"Just a squall," said the quartermaster, and some further terror must have shown in Gerald's face, because he laughed. "Want for me to tie a rope around your waist?"

"I think I'd like to go downstairs," said Gerald.

"I'd like a go at Cleopatra, but there you are," was the retort, and before Gerald could argue further, Cotton grabbed him around the waist, supporting him to move. He skidded and slid over the rainwashed wood and up the stairs with Cotton holding it up, toward the helm, and shoved him to sit on a storage bench a little ways behind the wheel.

"Best to stand where you can manage it, man," advised Thwaites cheerfully, his grip tight on the wheel, keeping their rudder steady and moving it in small increments – with the waves, Gerald thought. Thwaites had thrown his hat aside and tied his hair up in a higher bun, so that Gerald could see the constellations tattooed on the back of his neck. "You'll learn the dance soon enough."

"I'm going to be sick," Gerald threatened.

"It'll soon wash away," said Thwaites.

He wasn't sick.

The rain began to come down in hard, heavy sheets, water rushing hard over the decks, down the stairs, and although taking down the sails soothed it for a time, as the storm caught up the ship began to pitch far more wildly.

It made Gerald's stomach roil as the whole ship leaned one way and then the other, so much so that he felt as though he'd be thrown over the side if he fell too close to it. He was pitched at one point onto his feet even though he tried his best to seat himself, and at one point his feet almost went out from under him so that he went into the splits, but he managed to keep himself up with his hands wrapped around a railing.

It was hours later, when Gerald was soaked to his skin even through Thwaites' coat, that they finally went below decks again, and he walked on his own without anybody holding him up, although he kept stumbling and falling against the walls as they went, and he was shivering.

It was much warmer in the captain's cabin, which had two bunks, and Thwaites tossed him some towelling cloth. Gerald reached up to squeeze some of the wetness out of his hair, and when he pulled the towel away he heard himself squeak, because the captain had stripped off his wet clothes.

He was covered in tattoos and scars, and there was a huge bite around his calf that looked to be from a shark, but Gerald didn't examine it much. He was distracted by the comfortable size and gentle curve of the captain's—

"Stop ogling," said Thwaites. "Take those clothes off, you'll catch your death."

"I'm not going to strip off my clothes in front of you!"

"I'm sure the crew will be glad to help you if you don't want to do it in here," said the captain. "Shall I show you to the mess?"

Gerald was silent for a moment, and then clumsily undid the lacing on his chemise.

He should have been relieved that Thwaites didn't even look at him once his clothes were stripped off, but a part of him was disappointed, a dangerously and embarrassingly large part of him. Thwaites *had* flirted with him before – or at least, threatened his virtue – but now, he barely even looked at him, rifling through a cabinet before tossing him a long shirt and some loose cotton trousers.

"You're hungry, I hope," said the captain.

"Mr Poole should eat," Gerald said quickly as he pulled the shirt over his head. The sleeves were the right size, but it was far too big around his middle, and Thwaites took his belt from the clothes he'd been wearing, handing it back to him so that he could tighten it around the trousers. He looked as though he were wearing sacking, they so ruched and bundled around his middle, but there was no helping that: now that he *was* dressed, the captain was looking at him as though he were studying him, his eyes narrowed.

Inside and away from the red sunrise he'd been in this morning, Gerald saw that Thwaites' eyes were not the colour of honey, but were really hazel, a sort of molten mix of brown and dark green, and in the lamplight, the flecks of lighter colour shone in them, almost as though he had constellations on his irises as well as tattooed on his back.

"A good valet you are," he said thoughtfully. "Come."

They ate at one of the benches beside the captain and the quartermaster, and once Wicks had eaten his meal, Gerald took each of his arms, first the left and the other, and pressed his thumbs into where the rope had bit into them, where he'd bound. He'd done this quite a few times before over the years, and he knew how to rub and press so as to soothe the bite without making it bruise further.

Wicks didn't pull away from him, but he seemed uncertain of being touched, and he gritted his teeth slightly.

"Does it hurt?" asked Gerald.

"Some stiffness, Wicks," said Wicks. "That's all."

"Very well, Mr Poole," muttered Gerald, but pressed hard on the centre of the lieutenant's wrist, watching his face twist in pain. "If you're certain—"

"Your point is made, you don't need to belabour it," said Wicks sharply, and Gerald returned to his previous ministrations.

"You scratched yourself here," said Gerald, stroking the graze of skin to one edge of the inside of Wicks' wrist, although he hadn't drawn blood – the skin just flaked in places. "Did you catch yourself on a nail or something when you tried to loosen your bonds? It's always better to bend your elbows out a bit, you know – it makes it easier to get at the ropes, but you're also less liable to do this, especially if you move with your knees. You've more control that way, you see, than just rocking or something, because you're using your joints, but I suppose it doesn't make much difference when the ship is pitching one way and then the next."

Wicks was staring at him, a very queer look twisting his expression, but before he could say anything, Thwaites interrupted. "I've had your man above decks," he said pleasantly. "We'll make a sailor of your valet yet, Mr Poole."

Wicks said nothing, avoiding Thwaites' gaze and keeping his on Gerald, and Gerald began to massage his stiff upper forearm. He did it, of course, because he felt guilty that Wicks should be bound and abandoned on his behalf for so many hours – but there was a part of him that enjoyed it, enjoyed feeling Wicks' stiff, sailor's muscle relax under Gerald's hands.

Gerald'd been at sea a while, and he missed the touch of other people's skin.

"I am to sleep in that room?" asked Wicks.

"You are," agreed the captain.

"There is no reason my valet shouldn't sleep with me," said Wicks. He was good at being a gentleman, it seemed to Gerald – he was more convincing than Gerald would be himself.

"Hardly," said Thwaites. "Perhaps I want him in my bed – perhaps I want to entertain the crew with him."

Wicks was abruptly angry, his jaw setting, his hands clenching into fists, and the captain laughed; Gerald didn't know if all his threats were to be as empty as those he had made so far, but to soothe Wicks, he did say, "He's not harmed me."

"Good," rumbled Wicks.

Thwaites was looking at Wicks as though he were someone very impressive, very attractive indeed – and he was quite right, of course, but it was nonetheless a concern.

"You two will survive a night apart," said Thwaites. "One begins to wonder, Mr Poole, if it is possession or protection that motivates you, or perhaps just the fear that your valet will find he enjoys himself more with my crew than with yourself."

Wicks gripped Gerald's hand, interlinking their fingers, and Gerald inhaled; when Wicks brushed his mouth over the back of Gerald's knuckles, Gerald felt himself burn pink, and swallowed.

"If you're going to perform, at least show some leg," said Thwaites, sounding quite bored.

Gerald slept that night pinned between Thwaites and the wall of the bunk. He kept himself folded small, that they needn't touch, as the captain sat up and read by candelight, Cotton snoring softly in the bunk above their heads.

Gerald was cold, but he didn't try to broach the gap.

"Are you going to abuse me?" asked Gerald when the captain finally blew out the candle.

Thwaites was stifling a yawn in the darkness as he said, "You'll have to ask me more nicely than that."

“No. I mean— Is that why you brought me?” asked Gerald, and Thwaites sighed.

“Oh, hush,” he grumbled, and pulled Gerald closer. Gerald jumped, gasping, but Thwaites did nothing but hold him against his chest until he relaxed slightly into the heat of Thwaites’ body, and Thwaites dropped his grip. “Sleep,” he said. “I can’t be bothered arguing with you.”

He tried twice to escape – both times he was caught and hauled back into bed, and the second time, Thwaites laid on top of him. Thwaites had stripped down to his chemise for bed, and Gerald when he put his hands on Thwaites he could feel his skin, and he ached to feel more of it, to slide his hands up and under Thwaites’ shirt.

It was a pleasant weight, all muscle and heat, unspeakably pleasant: Gerald glowered from beneath him until he fell asleep himself.

* * *

As dawn came, Thwaites’ ship continued to pitch back and forth with the storm, and after an uneasy sleep, the Lamia’s navigator, a tall man by the name of Creed, came to let Jack free from his cell, and brought him into the mess.

He had heard the bustle as the shifts of sailors had traded over, and the room was filled now with the soft snores and soporific grumbles of men recently taken to their hammocks to sleep. Jack took the tack and ration Creed handed him with a quiet murmur of thanks, and stood a moment, looking at the sea of faces, many of them peaceably – some of them fitfully – asleep.

They were not, as on the Ambition, all white faces.

Many of them bore quite Mediterranean colouring, and walking amongst the crew this past day Jack had heard Portuguese and Spanish and Arabic spoken as sailors played cards or laughed together; there were Tamils like Thwaites, a handful of them; mixed in amongst these were men like Jack himself.

Pirate crews were motley by their nature – he didn't only see varieties of men's colours, but he saw men with various infirmities as well, missing legs or arms, missing eyes, and just as no man was uniform with the next, every one of them wore messy clothes unkempt, with no match of colour or article.

It made him itch, the way some of the men on the Lamia looked at him as he passed – Jack Wicks was loyal to the King, loyal to the navy his father had raised him to join, to lend his heart to, and here Jack was on a pirate vessel, looking at men who all deserved to be hanged, and perhaps saw him as more like them than like the navy men.

This was what his crewmembers decided they saw, he supposed, when they looked at him, no matter that he had never done a thing to earn his sentence.

He thought about Poole, naive and lily-white Poole with his wide eyes and blushing cheeks, his empty head – why, of all men, was it *him* that Jack should be saddled with? Him that he should decide to protect, to stand for, to decide that he should represent, what, a chance at gaining respect from officers who did not, would not, never would respect him?

But what if they would?

What if Poole made the difference?

He wondered if the other navy men thought of him as a molly, with what Cotton had joked about on the Ambition – the only way he might make his way out of this and back into naval service was if he brought both himself and Poole from this alive and well, that he might then be praised as rescuer.

Thwaites seemed to think that they had been fucking one another, or at least, that the Gerald Poole he saw in Jack Wicks was the sort to make use of his valet's body, and last night, when he had taken Poole's hand, it had seemed to make Thwaites draw back somewhat.

Wicks knew that he was—

Wrong, in that manner.

He knew that he was inclined to men as much as he was inclined to women, knew that the sight of a man undressed aroused a fire in him as much as a woman did, and no matter that he had never indulged this corruption of his nature, there remained feelings.

Gerald Poole was a handsome and beautiful creature, beguiling and with a constant smile, and Jack was not so foolish as to have not noticed his flirtation, the way that he looked at Jack – and saw was he so foolish as to reach for a forbidden tree and pull the fruit from it, the better to bring the garden crashing down.

But to touch Poole now was not simply a matter of indulging his wrongful desire for another man – to touch Poole now might protect him from these pirates and their own perverted natures.

Did that make it right? Did it make it moral?

When Poole came into the mess, he sped his gait to meet Jack more quickly, and at the roil of the deck beneath them he stumbled and fell: Jack caught him by the waist and pulled him into his lap, not dropping him to the floor, and allowed Poole to fall against his chest, catching his breath.

Jack gripped Poole tightly, one arm wrapping loosely around the curve of Poole's knee and the other around his lower back, and Poole shivered, but didn't pull away.

"He harmed you?" asked Jack.

"No."

"Good."

Thwaites, coming after Poole, stood for a moment before them, watching them with interest. His gaze lingered on Jack's hands, where they wrapped around Poole's body, where they held him close. "Your valet tells me you want to pick olives, Mr Poole."

"Have something against that?" asked Jack cautiously.

"A curious desire, that's all," said Thwaites. "For a young man of means."

"All desires are curious in the eyes of other men," said Jack. "It's the nature of the thing."

As Thwaites stepped away to speak with the boatswain, Poole whispered, "I'm sorry."

"No sense being sorry for the sins of other men," said Jack. "You're no Christ."

Poole leaned in closer, pressing his face into the side of Jack's neck, and Jack exhaled as smoothly as he could, shifting his grip on Poole's body as he felt Poole's chest against his own, one of his knees curling up against Jack's hip. His breath was hot on the juncture of Jack's shoulder, and Jack was ashamed at the way his body surged with delight at the sensation.

He'd been with women – had them kiss him and sit in his lap in taverns. He'd never gone to bed with one, never gone to bed with anybody, didn't want to carry some disease into his marriage bed or leave bastards behind him.

He would like a wife, one day, if he made it free and clear of this business – a wife, he expected, who would not clutch at him as Poole was clutching at him now.

"I don't think he means any harm," said Poole into Jack's neck.

"Not if it would lose him money," was Jack's thin-lipped reply. "But we should be killed immediately once either of us became a liability."

"Will they find us? The crew of the Ambition?"

"No."

"Oh. But, but we could esca—"

"No," said Jack. "Even were we to take one of the dinghies, we'd scarce make any headway before they noticed our absence, and even if we were free and clear of them, we would like as not to be found by others with no guarantee of safety before we met a shore. Once we make port, if there is no ransom paid, then we might think of escape."

"Oh," said Poole.

"We shall like as not make port soon, or they'll send some men to post for your ransom. If your family pays and pays fast, they shall let us free, I expect – we're more trouble than we're worth. If not, they'll kill us or make some play of us."

Poole hesitated. "You don't sound worried," he said.

Jack felt himself scowl. "I *am*," he said.

"Oh," said Poole. Was it the only thing the empty-headed idiot could say?

He sat back, and Jack looked at the expression on Poole's face. He looked more than terrified – there was a deep and palpable melancholy on his face, one that Jack could see that he was trying to hold back, his lips twisted as though he were on the very verge of tears.

Jack's fingers were brushing the soft skin of Poole's cheek before he even knew what he was doing, and he felt his hand stiffen, but didn't draw it back.

"It's no fault of yours," he said. "Nor mine. A situation like this is like the storm over our heads – we withstand it, or we die. No sense in taking blame."

"But they needn't have taken you as well as me," said Poole in a breathless whisper, and Jack's reply was a bitter noise.

"I could say the same," he said.

Thwaites' hand came in at the edge of Jack's vision, and Jack grabbed him hard by the surprisingly strong joint of a delicate-looking wrist before his fingers could curl in Poole's hair.

Thwaites, laughing, said, "So commanding. What a mighty king you shall be of your olive grove."

"Don't touch him," said Jack.

"Why not? He always seems to like it – attend."

Thwaites twisted his wrist free and stroked his fingers down the back of Poole's ear. The touch was delicate, barely brushing the flesh, and Jack could see it was teasing as it slid down the curve of his neck – Poole squirmed in Jack's lap, his knees pressed hard together, and Jack was disgusted by the way his own body surged to be involved, the way he wanted—

He resisted the sudden urge to tip Poole onto the floor.

"Your boy is very sensitive, Mr Poole," said Thwaites. "Do you starve him of touch to keep him keen, or is it some play of nobility on your part?"

Thwaites leaned in, kissing the shell of Poole's ear and making him jump: with Thwaites leaning in so close to the both of them, Jack could smell the scent on his clothes and dabbed on his neck, and it was a rosy, enticing one. "I'm no noble, lad," Thwaites murmured, his eyes meeting Jack's even as his tongue touched the skin of Poole's ear. "I would glut you before I starved you."

Poole's gulp was loud and audible, his throat jumping, and Thwaites laughed.

"You know, were he as well-used as I'm sure he'd like to be," said Thwaites, leaning back and looking at Jack as though Poole wasn't even there, was little more than furniture between them, "I expect a threat of danger would still perk him up. Curious little thing, is he not?"

Jack said nothing, but scowled.

"Yes," said Thwaites, inclining his head as though answering a question Jack hadn't asked. "That's not what does it for *you*, but I'll find what makes your cogs turn soon enough. Perhaps if I have your valet where you can see, you will respond accordingly?"

Poole squirmed again, a wriggling weight in Jack's lap.

"Do behave yourself," said Thwaites, and then he walked away.

"Get up," said Jack once he'd disappeared from sight, and Poole went to the bench beside him.

At the very least, this time, when Thwaites ushered Jack back into his brig, it was with a stack of books.

* * *

"Must you hold him captive, Captain Thwaites?" asked Gerald as he stumbled after the captain down the corridor and toward the stairs up onto the deck.

Thwaites' laugh came from low in his chest, one hand spread over his belly, and he was still laughing as he made his way up to the main deck, bending over slightly to keep laughing.

Gerald scowled at him, and Thwaites, seeing his ire, wiped a tear from his eye and simply shook his head, collecting himself amidst occasional chuckles as he led the way forward.

The storm had passed, and where the sun broke through the clouds, the soaked decks shone with its golden light. Gerald still slipped on it.

He had long resented being held in the confines of his cabin on the Ambition, and it bothered him immensely that Wicks should now be confined in the same manner, no matter that it was Wicks who had been his gaoler. The only person he'd really been permitted to assist with their duties on the Ambition had been the ship's cook, who now and then employed his assistance in plating things up that it might be done as quickly as possible – at other times, invariably, no matter how quiet or subtle he attempted to be in observing or engaging with another sailor's work, Second Lieutenant Wicks would be summoned and he would be led off and out of the way.

It wasn't like that on the Lamia, although he thought perhaps it ought be – he was a hostage, and yet even on his unsteady feet, he was permitted to walk up and down the top deck, seeing the sailors work. They had more discipline than he might have expected, working in easy harmony with one another, in rhythm as they worked, just as the men aboard the Ambition.

A sailor was a sailor, Gerald supposed, even before he was a brigand.

Mr Creed, the helmsman he had seen yesterday, took sight of him as he approached the ship's bow, and gestured widely. "What do you see?" he asked, posing the question as though it were one of some significance, and Gerald furrowed his brow, hesitating.

"A great deal of water and a blue horizon," he said, and Creed laughed. "Am I wrong?"

"No, no, you are right. But I meant here..." Mr Creed was working close with the carpenter, and the two of them were working on a section of deck that had been damaged last night, repairing the uppermost rail.

Gerald looked up to the ropes on the foremost mast, seeing their different colours, some more weathered than the rest.

"A pulley came loose in the wind, I suppose?" he asked. "And dashed the wood?"

Creed grinned. “That is right,” he said, sounding pleased. “And see you how you walk.”

“Like a colt on new legs.

“But walking!” Creed clapped Gerald so mightily on the back that for all their conversation about remaining upright, Gerald stumbled, but Creed caught him before he hit the deck and held him up, laughing.

Gerald, helpless to do anything else, laughed as well.

That evening, Thwaites asked, “How old are you?”

“Four and twenty,” said Gerald.

“And your master?”

Gerald realised his potential error all at once, and hesitated before he said, “He’s the same.”

“The same?” repeated Thwaites, as if giving him another chance.

Wicks had to be four and twenty – it was what Gerald’s papers said. “Yes.”

“Your master is very strapping for twenty-four.”

“Perhaps I just seem youthful,” said Gerald, “and he seems strapping in comparison.”

“Perhaps that is so,” said Thwaites, leaning back with his hands loosely folded over his belly, a faint smile curving his handsome lips.

When they left Thwaites’ office, it was with Wicks alongside them, and Gerald and Wicks were permitted to sit together and invited to play cards with a handful of other sailors.

Creed didn’t play, and nor did Thwaites, but Cotton joined the table with them.

Gerald won several rounds.

Gerald usually won at cards.

Even Wicks, who had observed him play before – albeit only for a few minutes before tearing him away from the table – seemed surprised.

Although Thwaites did not join them to play, after a while, he came over to observe.

Poker was the least interesting of the games, except perhaps for Rummy, and after a while, Thwaites came to lean over Gerald's shoulders, his hands resting on the table where they bracketed his body, his chin against Gerald's hair.

Wicks, sitting across from Gerald, scowled quite powerfully, but Thwaites' body was warm and he smelled very nice, and Gerald wasn't a fool – as much as this position allowed Thwaites to examine his cards, it allowed him to irritate Wicks in the same moment, and that was why he chose it.

"I'm not cheating," said Gerald.

"I see that," Thwaites murmured in his ear. Gerald had known he'd had sensitive ears, but he'd never had it utilised to such extent – when Wicks glared across at them, Thwaites dipped even more against Gerald's body, curling one of his hands in Gerald's hair, and Gerald sighed.

Wicks' scowl deepened.

"Are you bored, Justin?" asked Thwaites.

Gerald, resisting the powerful urge to be impolite, said, "No," and Thwaites laughed.

"We should bring him to Tortuga," said the fourth man playing with them, a heavily tattooed man named Carter, who had a lopsided haircut and was missing two fingers on his left hand. "He'd make more money there'n giving him back."

Wicks looked at him so coldly that Carter blanched.

"He'd get us all killed at that," observed Thwaites. "He's counting his cards.

As Cotton said, "What?" Gerald frowned, looking from his cards to the spread on the table, and then glancing askance up at Thwaites.

"He's doing mathematics in his head, working out the odds of the next card he picks from the deck," said Thwaites.

Gerald frowned deeper, looking at the faces of Wicks, Carter, and Cotton, before he looked back up at Thwaites.

"But we all are," he said. "That's how you play, isn't it?"

Thwaites folded his hands on top of Gerald's hand, leaning on them, and for once, he didn't laugh, but Cotton growled, "You little prick," and dropped his cards on the table.

Wicks had placed one of his hands over his mouth, his head tilted slightly to one side as he tried not to laugh, no doubt not wanting to give Thwaites the satisfaction, and Carter stared at the cards in his hands, then at the deck. "I don't get it," he said.

Gerald didn't get quite it either, but he didn't want to admit to that. He'd played cards an awful lot, in his time – he'd even been used in much the way Carter had suggested, set at a table to use his skills.

"Are we stopping?" he asked, aware he sounded disappointed.

"Try Whist," advised Thwaites.

"I like Whist very much," said Gerald. "The sailors on the Ambition didn't much care for it, I don't think."

"Another night," said Cotton, looking defeated.

"Did you know your valet could play like this?" asked Thwaites. His voice was soft and quiet and very deliberate, and Wicks, who had been pushing away his smile already, quickly schooled himself into pure neutrality to meet Thwaites' gaze.

"I don't play cards often," said Wicks. "Not even with Mr Wicks, I'm afraid."

Thwaites was curling Gerald's hair between his fingers, tugging and pulling gently on the strands, and it was a pleasant sensation, very soothing.

"You pick olives," he said.

"I don't," said Wicks smoothly, quickly, with pure ease. "But I would like to."

It was curious, watching Wicks take on an approximation of Gerald's identity – he did it with the ease of a man who had been playing other men his whole life through, and it felt like witnessing a dance, watching him and Thwaites back and forth with one another.

"How old are you?" asked Thwaites, and Gerald felt his mouth move, but he didn't let himself speak, tried not to even flinch.

"Four and twenty," said Wicks, once more unflinching, unblinking, as casual as a man could be – he was even packing the cards back together, and shuffling them idly. "I'll be twenty-five at the end of November."

Gerald's eyes fluttered closed as Thwaites gripped tightly to his hair with one hand and slid the other down the front of his shirt. Gerald stuttered out a breath, his head tipping back against Thwaites' chest.

Thwaites' slim fingers stopped where they touched his navel, brushing over the hair dusted on his belly, and Gerald bit out a grunt of sound, inhaling sharply through his teeth to keep from making any others.

Wicks' lip had curled, and the cards he had been shuffling were bending in his fingers.

"Perhaps if I distract him, he won't keep count," said Thwaites pleasantly.

"Does this amuse you?" asked Wicks. "Molesting a man who has no manner of escaping you?"

"It does," said Thwaites. "What's more, it seems to amuse him. Are you amused, Wicks?"

Gerald shook his head, but his cheeks were blushing brightly red and his skin was burning, and Thwaites' fingers were tickling over his belly in a way that made him shudder and jump, his cock so hard in his breeches he could barely stand it.

Thwaites' hand dipped lower, under his belt now, and he choked at the grip of his fine hand, his hips jumping.

"Captain," said Cotton exhaustedly as Gerald tried not to moan out loud, "we eat at these tables."

"Oh, you're right," said Thwaites, sighing.

"Wait—" Gerald complained, but Thwaites was already withdrawing his hand, and he curled his fingers instead back in Gerald's hair.

Wicks looked livid.

"Time for bed," said Thwaites, and Gerald rushed so quickly to his feet that he got tangled in the bench and almost fell over, but Thwaites pushed him back as soon as he tried to step after him, laughing merrily. "Let the valet sleep with his master tonight, won't you, Mr Cotton?"

At the dejected look on Gerald's face, Cotton laughed at him too, and he looked shamefacedly from the look on Wicks' own before it could bore into his soul and make a well there.

There would be enough of that tonight.

Part II

It was colder in the little room that had been set aside for Wicks' imprisonment than it had been in the mess, crowded as it had been with people, and as Cotton turned the key in the lock behind them, Jack saw that Poole huddled down slightly in his jacket, his arms wrapped around his chest.

He looked nervous when Jack approached him, but Jack ignored it, tilting up Poole's face with his hands on his cheeks to get a good look at his face. "Are you hurt?" he demanded, and Poole glanced away from Jack's face and down to the floor.

He shook his head, and Wicks inhaled softly, sliding his thumbs once more over the delicate skin of Gerald's cheeks before he drew his hands back.

"Take the lower bed," said Jack. "I can sleep on the top bunk, I doubt you'd be able to reach."

Poole watched him walk away – not that there was far to walk, in their little cell, its being small enough that Wicks could easily touch each wall with his arms outstretched one way, and could accomplish the same facing the other way by leaning one way and then the other – without saying anything at first, as Wicks unbuttoned his jacket.

Jack's skin was burning with a painful, indignant heat. Part of him, a part of him he was wholly disgusted with and quite ashamed of, had thrummed with need and desire at the way Poole had surged to meet Thwaites' hands, the way he'd wriggled under his touch.

What did that say of Jack Wicks, that he should see a man so molested, so abused, by a pirate captain, and that his cock should stir at the sight of it?

"Aren't you angry?" asked Poole in a small voice, and Jack glanced at him.

"Furious," he said, hearing the rumble in his voice. "Were it that I could do anything, sir, I would, but I can't – he's touching you to provoke me as much as to humiliate you, and were I to react more candidly, I'm sure it would make it worse."

Poole rocked forward slightly on his toes, and said, "You kissed my hand. And held me."

Jack felt as though he'd been plunged into ice water, and his stomach roiled as he looked back at Poole, at his pressed-together lips, his wide eyes. "I'm sorry," he said quietly, taken away with shame. "Better that they think us involved, I think, that we keep up the charade – I think it does serve to create some restraint in Thwaites, even to a minor extent. I do try to keep my touches chaste."

"You needn't," said Poole.

"I wouldn't debase you further," said Jack. "What I do now is enough."

"I'm not *debased*," said Poole, seeming abruptly very offended, and Jack looked at him in bafflement, at the sudden anger that curled his girlish lips, his eyebrows furrowing. "I'll have you know I've been touched far more openly and by far better-looking men than you *or* Captain Thwaites."

Jack, struck dumb, stared at him.

"I am handsome," said Poole, his lip curling further. "And I'm intelligent, too, far cleverer than any of you are giving me credit for – *lots* of men desire me, in the circles I walk about. Just because you don't doesn't mean I'm debased. I'm— I'm in demand, and desired. Not debased."

Jack turned his head sharply away, focusing on taking off his jacket to set aside, although he almost hesitated in undressing himself.

They'd said of Poole what he was, and Jack himself had seen Poole react to Thwaites' wandering hands, had heard Poole's flirtation – he *knew* that Poole was like as not a molly, and had known it, but... But it was one thing for a man to hold his vices, to carry them with him, and quite another to talk about them as though they were something to be *proud* of, something—

Natural.

As if what kept Jack from performing any sort of attraction for him was because he was not sufficiently handsome, and not that he was a man.

"Now are you angry?" asked Poole as Jack kicked off his boots.

"No," Jack said, almost whispered the word, although it was very loud in the little room.

"You could have fooled me," said Poole. "I'm not *stupid*."

"I don't recall saying you were."

"But you thought it," said Poole. "All of you, you thought about how stupid I was, no matter that I'd just wiped the floor with all of you at cards – if any of you could do what I do, perhaps you'd win. That's the only reason it pleases you to think I'm a fool, because you're deficient where I'm not."

"I did not call you deficient," said Jack irritably. "And nor did I call you stupid."

"Do you really not think me handsome?"

"It's not for me to say!" snapped Jack, turning to glare at him, and Poole withdrew somewhat, his large eyes almost filling with tears, as though he really were a girl, and Jack clenched his hands at his sides. "It's not *right*, asking me to... I'm no— I'm not like that. Like you. I would never."

"But you'd want to?" asked Poole, and Jack clenched his teeth.

"Just get in bed, Poole," he said.

Poole crossed his arms over his chest, his eyes glistening, and he drew up his head, drew himself to his full height, which wasn't very tall at all. "I wish he'd let me sleep with him," he said venomously, and Wicks wrinkled his nose in disgust, not knowing what to make of that.

"Bed," he repeated.

"Not alone," said Poole challengingly, taking a step forward. "It's too cold."

Jack released an irritated growl of sound, making to pull himself onto the second bunk, and Poole rushed forward. He wasn't strong enough to really shove Jack with any strength, but Jack didn't want the temptation of Poole's hands on him, didn't want Poole to touch him, to clutch at him, to...

He withdrew his hands right back, his wrists and his shoulders against the wall, and Poole stared at him, examined each part of his body where he had withdrawn himself from Poole's reach, and Poole looked angrier and angrier with the moments that passed.

"Is that why you've been so taciturn since first we made our acquaintance?" he demanded. "Because you didn't dare say a word to a molly, lest you encourage me?"

It was so incredibly, impossibly self-obsessed, utterly ignorant of the truth and of his surroundings and of Wicks as his own man, that Jack almost wanted to shout back at him exactly how stupid and foolish he was proving himself, but to reply would only encourage Poole further, and Jack didn't want to touch him.

The blows of Poole's fists against Jack's breast all but bounced away from him, Poole punching as hard as he could and making no impact whatsoever, and Jack said nothing.

"You're *frightened* of me," said Poole coldly, almost savagely, as though it were the worst insult in the world. "What, you think I'll overpower you? That I'll force you to touch me, to embrace me, to kiss me? As if I'd want you to. I expect you'd like me hanged."

When Jack still said nothing, leaning back against the wall, Poole's fury glittered in his teary eyes and glistened on the teeth bared by his snarl, which was anything but threatening. "I thought it was me," he hissed. "I thought it was— I thought it was me, that I was rude, or entitled, or too loud or irritating, and I felt so awful wasting your time that you had to act as nursemaid for some seasick rich boy who'd never done a day's work in his life, and you thought me a sodomite just *desperate* to—"

"Be quiet," said Jack, not wanting to hear any more of the self-pity, the *narcissism*, and Poole, in a move utterly unsurprising, actually stamped his foot on the ground.

"No!"

"Be—"

"No! No, I won't! I'll prove you right, shall I? My family is having me sent to some villa in the middle of some infinite olive grove like a sodomising minotaur, that everyone be spared the sight of me, and I'll pick olives instead of men's hearts!"

Jack leaned further back as Poole came closer, his elbows shoved up against Jack's breast, hands fisted in the lapels of his shirt.

"Because I'm not good at hiding it," he said furiously, wetly. "Because I'm not good at hiding anything! Does it please you, that I *am* stupid after all?"

Jack wanted to be sick. He hated that part of him was offended at Poole's misinterpretation, that he wanted to defend himself – that he wanted to say that no, Poole, it had nothing to do with you, my anger was with my situation, the treatment I received through no choices of my own, unlike the choices *you* made... He knew there was no point in it, that Poole would never understand, that he'd never try to, that he could never conceive of something not being about him, but *this*—

As if Jack hated him.

As if Jack would care what the fuck Poole thought of other men, if he only kept his hands to himself, if only he could shut the fuck up.

"If I wasn't hanged," said Jack, his mouth moving without his permission, "I would be discharged. They'd jump at the chance to discharge me already – hanging would be a certainty. A hard hanging, too, an executioner who would jump at the chance to make it slow and drag it out, the knot loose enough that I hung and choked instead of broke my neck, and very public, with a large audience. Not everyone, Poole, has a noble family backing his predicament, ready to pay for his retirement to some winery where tributes of young virgins might be sacrificed from a distance."

Poole's grip on his shirt loosened.

"And," Jack went on, "I might point out that my discharge from the navy is guaranteed regardless, because of the deception I played thinking it might prevent your kidnapping."

"Well," Poole said bitterly, "hasn't *that* worked a treat?"

"A moment ago you were talking at length about how you're not the sort of noble who would tantrum if he doesn't get his way," said Jack, "about how you went to such lengths not to inconvenience me. It seems to me now, Poole, that your colours are showing."

He said it very coldly, more coldly than perhaps he knew he was capable of, and Poole stumbled back and away from him.

"To bed, then," said Jack.

"Together," said Poole, and Jack's skin burned. "It's too cold."

"No."

"Why not?" demanded Poole. "You're to be discharged either way, you said."

"Whore yourself out all you like," growled Jack, gripping the top edge of the bunk and hauling himself up. "I'm not going to fuck you because you're upset our captor hasn't."

"I've not the least interest in being fucked by some sailor who thinks he's untouched and holy because he's too scared to fuck men even though he wants to," said Poole, and Jack whirled on him, but didn't pull himself down to face him. Poole was looking up at him, all defiance, his hands clenched at his sides. "You're worse than what I am – at least I know what I am. At least I'm not a coward."

"You've not the slightest idea what bravery is," said Jack. "Forgive me if I don't take accusations of cowardice very seriously when they're posed by a pink-lipped little boy who squeals whenever the ship tilts underfoot and cries for help if a parrot looks at him funny."

Poole stared up at him, and his teary eyes did not come over dry, but something in them hardened, and he set his emotion aside for a moment to ask, "Think about the colour of my lips a lot, do you?"

Jack almost choked, feeling his own cheeks burn although he knew they wouldn't colour, and he turned himself over on his side to face the wall, ignoring every attempt Poole made to cajole him and to climb up to the top bunk with them, which he couldn't manage, lacking a ladder.

Jack's fury lulled him into a sleep that came with tense and angry dreams.

* * *

Gerald laid for a long time in the darkness of the room, glaring at the wall, before he finally slept. It wasn't fair. None of it was fair, none of it was fair or right at all, that he simply couldn't be trusted to carry on the way he had been because they were just certain he'd be arrested or killed or something this time, just for having a bit of fun, just for *existing*.

If he lingered in the places where the appropriate people were, if he went to soirées with the family or attended business meetings or came into his father's shops and warehouses, he was doing the wrong thing – he was being too loud, too tactless, putting people off, no matter that he knew more about the trade than any of his brothers, no matter that whenever he was in the room they asked him before they asked each other because they knew he knew.

If he went to anywhere people might be fun, if, God forbid, Gerald went into places where people might like him – coffee and ale houses, silly little fairs, parties and circuses, *then* he was bringing everyone into disrepute just by being elsewhere.

The only thing he was good for was to be locked in an office, doing paperwork he couldn't stand, or lounging about in the house and getting into arguments with his mother, because even then, he was making too much noise.

What was the point?

And now, now, he was finally getting shipped off because they'd simply had enough of his doing the wrong thing, no matter that the wrong thing was always suspiciously similar to the *right* thing everyone had suggested he do ten minutes before, and it would be just the same.

He woke at the turn of the key in the lock, and he glared fiercely up at the bunk above his head. He'd shivered through the night, and what's more, he'd heard Wicks shiver too, no matter that with all that blubber and muscle on his body he *ought* have been warmer – talk about cutting off your nose to spite your face.

When the door opened, Gerald took to his feet, and walked with purpose, although not without glancing to make sure that Wicks was awake, and watching what he was doing.

He had to stand on his tiptoes to reach, but Thwaites' lips were warm and soft – he used some sort of butter on his lips, Gerald suspected, to keep them so lovely – and his beard bristles tickled Gerald's mouth.

He tried to lean further into it, tried to part his lips and invite Thwaites to kiss him more deeply, but Thwaites gently pushed him back with two fingers against Gerald's chest. He was smirking, his handsome lips curved into the smile, and he said in amused tones, "Good morning to you too, Mr Wicks. Might I assume you will pose a similar greeting, Mr Poole?"

Wicks, who was sitting up on the top bunk, his arms crossed over his chest – he was awkwardly positioned, too tall to sit up straight, and one of his legs hung over the side – rolled his eyes.

"Why would you want him to?" asked Gerald coolly, and Thwaites arched an eyebrow.

"Why indeed," he said richly. "Perhaps breakfast will soothe everyone's hurt feelings."

"I expect a stiff kick would too," muttered Gerald, making to step past Thwaites and into Thwaites' office, but Thwaites' hand shot out and kept him in place, preventing him from moving.

"Something tells me, Mr Poole," he said, addressing Wicks, "that our servant's devotion has been forgotten."

Wicks released an irritated harrumph of sound, and before Gerald could even think, let alone say a word, Thwaites had him twisted around and pinned against the door frame by his throat. He was more than on his tiptoes now, scrambling for purchase as he choked around the grip of Thwaites' handsome hand around his neck, and Wicks hit the floor like a solid weight as he jumped down from the bunk.

“I expect I can teach him a lesson,” Thwaites said, in casual tones, but he had to raise his voice over the sounds of Gerald’s choked, sharp noises of fear and protest – he had taken a dagger from his belt and was holding its honed blade directly in front of Gerald’s face, tilting the tip forward and toward his eye.

“Let him go,” said Wicks sharply, “let him go, Thwaites, it’s nothing—“

“Nothing?” repeated Thwaites innocently, tapping the flat of the blade against Gerald’s cheek, and Gerald let out a whimpered sound when he tilted it, so that its sharp edge met his cheekbone. “Mr Poole, why, the disrespect, the brattiness – this is hardly becoming of a good valet, is it? Should I cut out his tongue?”

The blade dropped to Gerald’s mouth, clinking quietly against his teeth, and Gerald’s eyes overflowed with tears – he’d managed to hold back last night, prevented them from brimming over with sheer anger, but there was no anger now, only terror, and his tears were wet on his cheeks. He tried not to sob because it made his lips quiver and his tongue jump, and the tip of the dagger’s blade was very cool and surprisingly heavy against his lower lip.

“Please,” said Wicks.

“Please?” Thwaites repeated softly, and still, he wasn’t looking at Gerald, was keeping his gaze on Wicks and treating Gerald as though he almost wasn’t even there, even as Gerald tried to kick his feet underneath him and stop the constriction on his throat, terrified to move his head unless the blade cut him.

“I do entreat you, Captain Thwaites,” said Wicks seriously, “please let him go.”

Thwaites withdrew the blade before he dropped the grip he had on Gerald's throat, and Gerald dropped hard onto the floor. He buried his face in his hands, his knees drawn up in front of him: he was breathing heavily, hauling in gasps so ragged that they cut at his bruised throat, and his head was spinning, his heart thumping in his chest. He couldn't stop himself from sobbing, rocking in his place on the floor, and Thwaites, to Gerald's startled horror, crouched beside him.

"There there, Mr Wicks," he said softly, his expression showing no regret, but no cruelty either, as he pushed Gerald's hands away and stroked his thumbs through the tears on Gerald's cheeks. "No harm done."

Gerald was sniffling as Thwaites proffered his handkerchief, and he took it quickly, hurrying to wipe it over his cheeks.

"Treat your toys better, Mr Poole," said Thwaites in a voice as thick and sweet as molasses as he stood to his feet, tugging Gerald up with him. His hands moved over Gerald's rumpled clothes, now, straightening his blouse and his jacket, and the tenderness wanted to make Gerald sob anew, but he managed to hold himself back. "Or someone might think you don't want them any longer."

Gerald inhaled reedily, trying his best not to cry any more, and he risked a glance at Wicks, whose skin had a chalky pallor to it, glistening with anxious sweat, and whose expression was a mask of scarce restrained anxiety.

"Come join us in the mess once this little drama is concluded," said Thwaites, and his boot heels tapped on the floor as he walked out into the corridor.

A few seconds of silence ticked by between them as Gerald tried to catch his breath, rubbing at his sore throat and swallowing down his tears. He looked a mess, he knew, even after he'd wiped his eyes clean and blown his nose, and Wicks just stood there and watched him.

"Are you alright?" he asked finally.

"As if you care," muttered Gerald, and made to follow the captain.

They sat elbow to elbow in the mess, only because when Wicks sat beside him, Gerald made to get up, and Mr Cotton grabbed him by the hair and shoved him back down again.

“I begin to dislike you, Mr Cotton,” said Gerald.

“That’s good,” said Cotton good-naturedly. “I like a head start.”

The day passed in tense and irritable silence, the two of them made to sit on the top most deck beside the helm – whenever Gerald attempted to wander off and observe the crew, as he was ordinarily permitted, someone would usher him back again, and perhaps they’d have done the same to Wicks if he’d only bother to move.

“Such a sad thing,” said the captain merrily from the helm, his hat pinned into his hair, his handsome brown skin shining almost like gold in the morning sun, “when two young boys come to quarrel.”

“We aren’t quarrelling,” said Gerald, at the same time Wicks said with some anger, “We’re not *boys*.”

Gerald glared at Wicks, who didn’t even do him the respect of returning his hard look, and when Gerald got to his feet, a passing gunner shoved him down again.

Thwaites looked back at them wryly before turning back to the sea. “Ah,” he said, with some cheer. “To be young again.”

“As opposed to very old, like Greybeard,” muttered Gerald under his breath.

Thwaites turned his head back to retort, but before he could, it was Wicks that smacked him upside the head, and hard.

“*Ow*,” said Gerald plaintively.

"Hold your tongue before I hold it for you," growled Wicks, and Gerald leaned back from him, his cheeks burning. Wicks held his gaze for a second before he, too, seemed slightly embarrassed, and turned the other way, so that they were at angles facing away from one another on the bench.

"I begin to see why so many of my headmasters abandoned the occupation," remarked Thwaites to Cotton, who laughed.

"If we are boys, Thwaites, that makes you Laius of Thebes," said Wicks.

"Oh," said Gerald coolly, "how well read he is."

"You think I won't strike you again?"

"Strike me harder. See if I care."

"Why, the better to pleasure you, perverted creature that you are?"

"*You* can pleasure *me* by drowning."

Wicks leaned in toward him, eyes hard, but Gerald didn't budge. "You first," said Wicks.

"I'll go right now."

"Will you?"

"Of course," snapped Gerald, leaning in closer, so that his nose almost brushed Wicks. "I will throw myself from this vessel and let myself drown, all the better to please you – unless of course, so *bound up* as you are with duty, Second Lieutenant, feel compelled to rescue me?"

Behind them, Gerald was aware of Cotton loudly sighing, and the sound of a flint lighting.

As the captain lit up a cigarillo, leaning up against the rail – Mr Cotton had taken the helm from him – Cotton muttered irritably under his breath, shaking his head, although he wasn't muttering loud enough that Gerald could hear.

"A bet is made with two parties, Paul," said Thwaites.

"Seems the parties are more often yours than anyone else's, Ced. Left pocket."

"Thank you," said Thwaites. As Gerald and Wicks both stared, Thwaites blew out a small cloud of dark smoke, and reached into Cotton's pocket with the familiarity of one who did it often, fishing out three coins.

"A pleasure doing business with you, as always, Mr Cotton," said Thwaites, leaning in close to almost murmur the words in Cotton's ear, threatening to put his hand in his pocket again.

A part of Gerald was almost jealous, until Cotton staunchly replied, "Go get fucked by an octopus."

"What?" asked Gerald as Thwaites looked down at them, and Thwaites took another slow drag of the cigarillo before he exhaled more smoke, the sound of it an indulgent sigh.

"Pray," he said, sort of airily, as though he was trying to hold back his laughter before he told the punchline, "of the two of you, valet and gentleman, which holds the rank of Second Lieutenant?"

"Oh, fuck," said Gerald.

"Hell's bells," muttered Wicks, and put his head in his hands.

"Are *you* called Justin, sir?" asked Thwaites.

"No, sir," said Wicks defeatedly. "My name is John William, sir."

"And are you a Johnny or a Bill – your last name is Wicks, I take it?"

"It is, sir, but I'm neither a Johnny nor a Bill. I'm a Jack, sir."

"Very good," said Thwaites, and looked expectantly to Gerald.

"Well," he said sharply. "You know my name."

"You lied to me," said Thwaites, shrugging his shoulders. "Perhaps, young man, I'm wounded."

"You lied about your name," said Gerald, and Wicks turned his head to glance at him, even as Thwaites frowned and furrowed his brow.

"I did no such thing."

"You told me your name was Orion Thwaites, as it says in your logbook, but he just called you Ced."

"And were your Christian name *Orion*, young man, I expect you'd go by your middle name as well."

"I'd choose to either use it or not, but if I did use it, I'd not tattoo it on the back of my neck."

Thwaites opened his mouth, then closed it. "Well," he said to Cotton, "we know the young man is not an astronomer."

Cotton laughed.

"The constellation on my neck is not Orion, Mr Poole, it is the Argo, and the one over my heart, if you were interested, is Pisces."

Interrupting this conversation, apparently bored of it, Wicks demanded, "Did you bet money on how long we'd keep up our deception?"

"We did," grumbled Cotton.

"Mr Cotton had faith in the two of you that you'd keep up your deception for three days and nights," said Thwaites, curling one of his hands around Cotton's shoulder, and Gerald watched the way Cotton didn't draw away, barely even reacted, apparently so used to his casual, affectionate touch. Something in him stirred. "I flatter myself, however, that I know two hot-headed young idiots when I see them."

"You knew?" asked Gerald. "From the very beginning?"

"My dear child," said Thwaites, "you have hands so soft that you might have been born yesterday, and whilst I confess, the handsome hue of your skin makes it difficult to discern a sailor's tan in you, Mr Wicks, you are more than at home upon a ship, and one can see in your eyes your knowledge of the vessel about you and its workings. If anything, Second Lieutenant sounds like a curiously *low* rank for you to be in possession of."

Wicks set his jaw. "Why bother, then, in taking both of us?"

"Leverage, as I told you from the outset," said Thwaites. "And I rather wanted to tie one of you up, but I couldn't possibly tie up a gentleman."

"Yes, you could," said Cotton.

"Alright, yes, I could," said Thwaites. "But what a joy it was to see you wriggle your way out of it, Mr Wicks – we shall try Poole next, and see how he fares."

Wicks raised his head, sitting very straight upon the bench. "You're to kill me, then," he said, and Gerald, alarmed, jumped to his feet and stood at Wicks' shoulder, between him and Thwaites.

"You mustn't," he said. "I won't allow it."

Thwaites, almost leaning on Cotton now, the two of them touching at the shoulder although they faced opposite directions, took a thoughtful drag of his cigarillo. After puffing out his smoke, he asked, "Could you have been a headmaster, Paul?"

"It would depend," said Cotton, "on if I still had possession of a flintlock pistol."

"I don't think so, Paul."

"Then no, Ced, like as not, I couldn't've."

"How old are you, Lieutenant Wicks?"

"Nine and twenty, sir," said Wicks. "Almost thirty."

"Very good. I'm very glad neither of you is called Justin – not the sort of name a man can cry out in ecstasy. Now, Mr Poole."

A loaded pistol was pointed into Gerald's face, and he froze, gulping hard. He didn't pull away from Wicks, but leaned further in front of him, one of his hands on Wicks' shoulder.

"Do you care to elaborate," asked Thwaites in slow and deliberate tones, "on that Greybeard comment you made a moment ago?"

"You're going to throw away all that ransom money over a comment on the grey in your hair?" asked Gerald, trying not to let his voice quaver, and failing.

"I would be no poorer than I am right now," said Thwaites dangerously, the constellations gleaming like hot honey in his eyes, "and last I checked, there *is* no grey in my hair."

"You need a new mirror, then," said Gerald. "The silver at your temples shines very obvious in the light."

"Christ's mother, Poole," hissed Wicks, "would you sit *down*?"

"If he wants to shoot me over vanity, let him," said Gerald, and for all he was shaking like a wet poodle, he didn't break his gaze away from Thwaites for even a second. He didn't even feel like crying, although he was fairly certain things might be different had he not been crying an hour before.

Thwaites' frightening scowl became a sly smile, and he lowered the gun.

"See how steady he is, Mr Cotton?" he asked as he put it away.

Relieved beyond measure and quite surprised to be alive, Gerald felt his knees go weak, and he fell back into Wicks' lap.

Cotton, facing the other way, said, "No," very pointedly.

Gerald expected Wicks to shove him out of his lap, back onto the bench, but he didn't, keeping a loose grip around Gerald's middle to hold him steady.

"Do you think me very stupid?" asked Gerald miserably as Thwaites descended the stairs.

Wicks gave him a nasty look. "Well, I don't think anyone for miles thinks you smart."

"You didn't realise I'd called you the wrong thing until he said," said Gerald. "So it's not just me."

"Of course I did!"

"Liar."

Wicks leaned back from him, lip curling. "*Molly*."

"I am, so it happens. What are you, a virgin?"

Wicks' face whipped directly to the side, almost as though Gerald had slapped him, and Gerald crowed out a noise of victory.

"Point to Poole, I think," said Cotton.

"Must you listen?" demanded Wicks, irritable, but Gerald felt – and he did feel – that he wasn't irritable all over.

"'Til your bickering nonsense renders me deaf," said Cotton. "Not to worry, I feel the levee is soon to break."

"Get off me," said Wicks, shoving Gerald onto the bench, but then he leaned forward like a schoolboy to hide his excitement, and Gerald laughed at him as he pressed his knees hard together.

"Not to worry, lad," said Cotton. "There's many a man older'n you who's yet to get his cock wet."

"No there isn't," said Gerald.

A moment passed.

"Aren't you going to argue with him?" Wicks asked, sounding almost hopeful, and it was really so sweet and genuine that Gerald almost felt guilty, except that he didn't.

"Tried my best," said Cotton breezily, not sounding sincere at all, and whilst turning his face away to keep from meeting Gerald's gaze, Wicks crossed one of his legs over the other.

* * *

Poole, predictably, began to chatter after a few minutes of silence, and Jack sat apart from him, leaned slightly forward even after his erection had calmed itself and was no longer a visible bulge in the front of his trousers. It was humiliating beyond measure, for a man his age to react so to a man in his lap – a skinny, infuriating, unbearable piece of fruit, at that.

Poole didn't look at Jack, looked away from him quite intentionally, and asked Cotton question after question.

"Have you been sailing very long?"

"Since I was nine."

"You like it?"

"I'm a sailor. Don't know it ever occurred to me to like it or not. It's what I do."

"Do you like being at the helm?"

"On a day like this, sure enough. Nice, clean waters, warm sun, good wind in our sails. Not much fun in a squall like yesterday."

"Mr Creed seemed to like it."

"Mr Creed'd enjoy if we sailed into a maelstrom."

"What's the worst storm you've ever been in?"

"Edge of an hurricane. We were sailing to Port Royal, and the squall as ran over us was like nothing you've ever seen – waves was higher than palaces, the sky so grey it was purple, kept cracking across with lighting. We got turned right over, twice, were wrecked on some nameless island. We'd lost two masts of four, and half the hull – not to mention half the crew. We were wrecked two months before a French navy ship came by, and a rescue made. That was when we were merchants still."

"What did you trade in?"

"Whatever was selling. Spices, silks, powder, iron."

"Did you enjoy that?"

"It was a job."

"Do you like this better?"

"Until now."

"What's different now?"

"You won't stop fucking talking."

Jack sniggered, and ignored Poole's indignant look, looking to Thwaites as he came back up to the helm.

"Are they behaving?" he asked.

"No," said Cotton. "Don't know that they know how to behave, not in each other's company. *He* won't shut up, and he won't say a fucking word, but at least they're not sniping at each other any longer."

"Well, what's a bit of misbehaviour between handsome young men?" asked Thwaites, and cupped Poole's cheek. Poole looked up at him, leaning into his palm like a dog pleased to be pet by its master, and when Thwaites reached for Jack's face to touch him in the same manner, Jack caught him by the wrist and held him fast.

"Would you prefer I use my mouth?" asked Thwaites in a soft purr.

There was an allure in him. It was a dangerous allure, Jack could see that – Poole wanted to be fucked, that much was clear in him, was pleased to be made use of, treated as a girl, but Thwaites wasn't girlish in the least, and Jack didn't know what to make of him. He was genteel and calm and collected, seductive and smooth, and Wicks pressed his feet down against the deck surface to keep from clenching his hands or his jaw.

"I'd prefer you keep your distance," said Jack.

"It's a small ship."

"It's big enough," Jack replied, and Thwaites put his second hand on Poole instead, sliding his thumb down the length of Poole's throat, pressing delicately on his Adam's apple and, when Poole smiled, Thwaites smiled back.

Thwaites' fingers were tracing over the dark red marks he'd left earlier on – Poole was so ridiculously pale that he bruised as easily as anything, and there was a ring of burgeoning bruising where Thwaites had gripped him earlier.

And yet, here Poole was, spreading his legs, parting his lips, inviting Thwaites to fuck him, Thwaites who only this morning had lifted him by his throat and threatened to jam a dagger down his throat.

Jack was powerless to do anything more than watch in disgust.

When Poole reached to touch Thwaites back, reaching for his belt, Thwaites took him by the wrists and turned his hands over, facing them up toward the sun. He slid his thumbs over Poole's palms, squeezing and pressing on the meat there, and it made Poole sigh as though this, too, were pleasurable.

Thwaites was massaging Poole's hands, almost, his thumbs pressing and squeezing and making Poole wriggle a little, and Jack wondered what it felt like.

"You mean to tell me you'll pick olives with these hands?" asked Thwaites.

"I like olives," said Gerald.

"You've never picked olives before, though. It's all very well eating something, young man, but harvesting it is another matter," said Thwaites. "What was it you used to occupy yourself with before this, hm? Cards and whorehouses?"

"Men," said Poole, with a spiteful look at Jack, and Jack rolled his eyes.

"Any hobbies beside cock and poker?"

"I paint some," said Poole. "Play the harpsichord, a little, and the harp. Hunt – with traps and tracking, not on horseback. And I like to knit, though I'm no good at sewing."

"You can skin a rabbit?" asked Thwaites.

"Yes."

"Pluck a bird?"

"Of course."

"Scale a fish?"

"Yes," said Poole, and Jack watched him for a few moments, somewhat surprised. In all the chatter he had heard from Poole these past weeks, none of this had come up. He found it difficult to imagine Poole sat quietly at an instrument or getting on with knitting, let alone committing himself to being so useful for a few minutes that he could scale a fish.

Poole shivered as Thwaites pressed down on his palms.

"Were you very badly behaved at school?" asked Jack, wanting to interrupt this back and forth before it went on, and Poole gave him a scornful look.

"I was often conspicuously absent, actually."

"What, bent over behind the garden sheds?"

"At least I *went* to school," said Poole, and Jack raised his eyebrows.

"I think you just said you didn't," said Jack.

Thwaites turned back, and asked, "Is it charming or irritating, Mr Cotton?"

"Irritating," said Cotton. "But I don't want to fuck either of them, so perhaps I'm biased."

"Not even me?" asked Poole, and when Cotton shot him a funny look, Jack muttered, "Good God."

"Oh, he's *charming*," said Thwaites. "It's sweet." His hands were moving up Poole's wrists, playing over the delicate flesh there and making Poole shiver. "Want to kiss me?" asked Thwaites.

"Of course," said Poole, and Jack pressed his lips fast together.

"But you think I'm old?"

"Not as old as Mr Cotton."

Cotton threw a nasty hand gesture over his shoulder, and this made Thwaites laugh very loudly – he had an astonishingly loud and joyful laugh, when something really amused him, and there was something very beautiful in it, the way he gave himself over to the laughter when it took hold of him. He'd tip his head back, showing the tattooed lines of his handsome throat, his silken hair bouncing with the movement and making it shine in the light, including the grey that showed at his temples.

Jack looked away as Thwaites took Poole by the cheeks and kissed him. It was a hard and bruising kiss, open-mouthed and aggressive and clearly audible as he backed Poole up onto the bench, Poole moaning softly into Thwaites' mouth. Thwaites' hands were sliding further up Poole's arms, and Poole's hands at first ran clumsily all over Thwaites' chest, but when they went to the buckle of Thwaites' belt, Jack interrupted.

"Not in broad daylight," he hissed, slapping Poole's hands away. "At the damned helm."

"Doesn't it satisfy you dictating that I can't touch you, no matter that you want me to?" demanded Poole. "Why decree I can't touch him either?"

"It seems without my restraint you'd touch every man you saw," growled Jack. "No wonder your family need to exile you to an olive grove – your appetite is a menace."

Poole scoffed, not seeming as hurt as Jack had hoped, and retorted, "But not allowing so much as a hand down your trousers, that's normal, is it?"

Thwaites asked, "Do I take your objection to mean, Mr Wicks, that in the privacy of a cabin, you should be content were I to bugger young Mr Poole here to kingdom come?"

Jack looked at him disgustedly, and Thwaites smiled at him. He had thickly lashed eyes, some of the thickest eyelashes Jack had ever seen, and Jack bit down the disgust he felt with himself for noticing.

"Hm," said Thwaites. "Curious, that. What if I let you watch?"

Jack set his jaw.

"Cedric," started Poole, and Thwaites gripped him hard by the jaw.

"Ah," he said, as though scolding a pet. "No, I don't think you've earned that."

"What if I—"

Poole caught him by the hand before he could go for Thwaites' belt loop this time, and Poole let out a childish groan of frustration at the denial.

"If you exercised," said Jack, "perhaps you'd have healthier appetites."

"My appetite is tremendously healthy, thank you," said Poole coldly.

"I don't know," said Thwaites in mild tones. "I think your second lieutenant here might have a point."

"Point?"

"Oh, Mr Creed!" called Thwaites over his shoulder, and Mr Creed, the tall helmsman, came to stand on the stair, leaning against the bannister and taking in the scene.

"Hullo, Captain," said Creed.

"Hullo, Creed. Are you very busy?"

"Always, Captain."

"You are a consummate pedagogue, are you not, Mr Creed?"

"My grandmother was a pedagogue, Captain: I am just an educator."

"Would you like to educate young Mr Poole?"

"Which one?" asked Creed, and although Jack managed to hold back his surprise, Poole's face fell.

"I believe they've stopped trading faces for now," said Thwaites. "In any case, I believe Mr Poole should like to be educated in almost everything."

Jack frowned slightly, watching the expression on Poole's face, disbelieving and strangely eager as he looked between Creed and Thwaites.

"In sailing, you mean?" he asked, getting to his feet. "And— and carpentry, and rigging, and all that?"

"I'll teach you to swab the deck first," said Creed.

"Alright," Poole agreed readily, and Jack resisted the urge to roll his eyes. "Now?"

"Do you know what swabbing the deck *is,* Poole?" asked Jack.

"Yes, of course, but that doesn't mean I know how to do it," said Poole. "Properly, I mean, so it works and keeps the wood right, and to make up what you swab it with, and what exactly you use to— oh."

Jack was on his feet, his hand fisted in the back of Poole's jacket to keep him from following Creed.

"You can't make him swab the deck," he told Thwaites.

Thwaites blinked, his beautiful eyelashes seeming even more exaggerated by the expressive movement. "I'm sure I could," he said, "but I don't need to. He's raring for the off, as you can see."

"But— but you *can't*," said Jack, imagining passing back Poole and showing him worked to the bone and tanned, imagining how the fuck he might explain it to whatever commander interrogated him as to his conduct whilst supposedly protecting this hostage in the name of the king, the ways he'd be *blamed.* It was one thing if they set him to work – he knew how to work, wouldn't be wrecked by it, and no one would give a fuck about it, but Poole? "He's a gentleman," said Wicks. "You can't just put him to work."

"I like work," said Poole.

"See?" asked Thwaites. "He likes work."

"You don't want me to fuck, you don't want me to work, what am I meant to do?" demanded Poole, whirling to glare up at him. "Do you want to hang me on a shelf in a glass casement?"

"Your hands will be sore," said Wicks. "You'll cut them, get callouses, work them raw."

"I'll get used to it."

"You'll tan in the sun."

"Like everyone else."

"You—" Wicks inhaled, and set his jaw, clenching his hands at his sides. He looked at Poole, pale Poole with his frail features, thin as a rake, scared of parrots and liable to come over dizzy and ill in the face of little more than a mildly aggressive swell. "Forgive me for saying so, sir, but you aren't fit for this. My orders when you were assigned to my charge were to keep you safe and well, not have you crawling on the deck and hurting yourself, playing at being a sailor."

It will affect me too, he almost said, and didn't. Don't you understand, you arrogant, self-absorbed little toff? Don't you understand that I'll be held accountable for the condition I return you in, assuming we get out of this alive?

"I won't forgive you," pronounced Poole. "You prick."

“Mr Poole, I just want to—“

“No, I’m *bored*,” Poole said plaintively, dragging himself out of Wicks’ grip. “I’ve gone fifteen years without a nanny, I hardly need one now.”

Jack, powerless, could say nothing more, although at least he thought he saw the barest sign of guilt on Poole’s face, twisting his lips, before Poole rushed after Creed, almost skipping to follow him.

“You really want to swab the deck?” asked Creed.

“If you tell me how,” said Poole eagerly.

“You’re a funny one,” said Creed, patting him on the back, and they walked further down the deck.

“Let’s you and I go down to my office, Mr Wicks,” said Thwaites. “No sense worrying yourself up here that Mr Poole might get a splinter.”

“I’ll be blamed for how he comes back,” said Jack. “If you want someone to work, let me work – I can pull more than enough weight for each of us.”

“But it’s not you who’s desperate to do so,” said Thwaites softly, spreading his beautiful hands.

Every inch of him was beautiful – not in a girlish way, not in the way Poole was pretty, but in a noble way, beautiful in the way of a statue – beautiful in the way you imagined the subject of those statues must have been, before they were wrought in bronze or marble. There was a sense of eternity in Thwaites’ charisma and his beauty, as if it would last long after all of them were gone.

"You mean to return us for a ransom," said Jack. "Return *him* for a ransom – me, I'm just extra cargo. But after we are returned, after the bounty is paid, it's me who'll pay the further price. I'll be blamed for everything awry on his person, for a crease on his shirt, a hair out of place, let alone scars and sunburns and exhaustion, particularly if I, in comparison, seem untouched. Is that what brings you pleasure, Captain Thwaites? To bring that fragile creature to ruin, and know I'll suffer the consequences?"

"It does occur, Mr Wicks," said Thwaites deliberately, "that it is not yet decided that I should let you live at all. As you say, you're not needed for the ransom we'll demand. Perhaps you'd rather I run you through and toss you overboard now?"

"You might as well," said Jack. "If I don't die on this deck, and you work him like a mule, I'm liable to be quietly discharged, set aside – and I won't take another commission, even on a merchant ship. I'd be lucky to get work as a labourer. So yes, why not kill me? Let Poole call me a hero when he goes ashore, if he remembers my name to do so, rather than let him ruin my life more than he already has."

Thwaites leaned back against the rails beside the helm, watching Jack a moment, and Jack slowly sank back down to the bench, looking between Thwaites and Cotton both.

"My father," said Thwaites, "was a merchant trader. He sold tea and spices, ferried them from Madras home to England – and ferried my mother, as well. Such a price he paid to put me on ships for my education as a sailor – they all thought I was quite mad, hot-blooded, a young and bestial thing. Blamed everything they could on me – although admittedly, I was never as buttoned up and well-behaved as you seem to be. My colleagues rarely had to make things up to blame on me, as I'd done rather a few things worth bringing up."

"Captain Thwaites," said Jack, "if you believe I am even remotely interested in your attempts at empathising with my situation, you are very wrong."

"I'm not empathising," said Thwaites pleasantly. "I am pointing out that you aren't the only handsome young man to serve at sea alongside men who despise your mixed blood."

"And how that soothes me," said Jack coldly, "knowing that if Poole casts my life into ruin by virtue of working himself to the bone, that there are like as not other men much like me suffering on other ships."

"He is dramatic, isn't he, Paul?"

"Pot, black," replied Cotton. "Kettle, black."

"Why am I alive?" asked Jack.

"What an excellent question," said Thwaites. "One for the philosophers."

"I'm not asking the fucking philosophers," said Jack. "I'm asking you, the man who didn't kill me."

Cotton laughed quietly, and when he turned his head to glance back at Jack, Jack saw the glitter in his eyes, the curve of his mouth. He didn't actually look all that much older than Thwaites – they were each of them, Jack would guess, in their late forties, perhaps their fifties, but they looked healthy for it, made hale from keeping at their sailing life.

"You like him," said Thwaites.

"I like hearing someone else tell you you're a fucking prat," said Cotton. "It's only natural."

"We've known one another quite a while, Paul and I," said Thwaites. "Since we were but young men – a little younger than Poole, I was."

"I hope you're not keeping me alive because you think I'm going to let you fuck me," said Jack, and Thwaites' lips curved into a deeper, more dangerous smile, his eyes glittering.

"It occurs, Lieutenant Wicks, that your *letting me* might not be my biggest concern," Thwaites replied, and Jack repressed the urge to swallow around the lump in his throat. "Perhaps I don't want to fuck you, in any case – perhaps I simply want to fuck your man Poole where you can watch."

"He's not my man," said Jack. "And nor am I his. Captain Lewisham was asked to ferry him, and to humiliate me, he all but assigned me his batman – said that if even the tiniest thing upset their treasured guest, I should be whipped for it, and held to account."

"You've taken duty rather far," said Thwaites.

"Is it duty for a man to tread water instead of drowning?" asked Jack. "Is it duty for a man to look away from cannon fire or pistol shot? To stamp out a fire instead of letting it burn him alive?"

"Is that what Poole is to you? An anchor about your neck? Perhaps I should kill him now."

"And kill me with him," said Jack. "Because if he dies, I've no defence at all."

"There's something to be said for optimism," said Thwaites. "Even if we sent you back in the best of conditions, well-fed, well-rested, Poole with a handsome ribbon around his neck, do you really think they'd hail you as a hero?"

Jack crossed his arms over his chest, and said nothing.

"Not an optimist, then," said Thwaites.

When he led the way this time, albeit with reluctance, Jack followed him down below decks, and sat aside in his office as Thwaites did his paperwork.

* * *

The skies were darkening overhead when Gerald finally limped down the stairs.

He was sunburnt, his shoulders ached, his lips were chapped, and his fingers were stiff from gripping the brush; sweat soaked him down to his skin, his shirt transparent, and his hair was stuck wet to his head.

"Have a nice day?" asked Thwaites, at the same time as Wicks, visibly horrified, looked at him and said, "Good God."

"Yes," said Gerald. "Thank you."

"Bet you're hungry," said Cotton.

"Starved," said Gerald, and responded with profuse thanks as Cotton pushed him a bowl of stew.

"I don't know what you were worried about," said Thwaites to Wicks. They were each half-finished with their meals as Gerald ate greedily, surprised by how much his body suddenly craved nothing more than to eat as much as possible. "He seems a great deal happier now."

"He looks destroyed," said Wicks.

"Well, he isn't actively begging for cock," said Thwaites. Around a mouthful of salted pork, Gerald made to speak, but Thwaites interrupted him and said, "Yes, Poole, we assumed you'd still like some. Keep eating."

Gerald chewed and swallowed.

After they were through eating, Wicks said, "Give me your hands," and Gerald hesitated before he did, hissing when Wicks commenced to press and rub at his aching palms, rubbing the soreness from his fingers. It hurt quite a bit, but there came a relief after Wicks finished with each section he massaged, doing what Gerald had done to him before.

Wicks seemed to notice for the first time the scars on Gerald's wrists – not from cuts, for the most part, but from places where he'd previously been tied and the ropes had cut the flesh, and up toward his elbow, one ugly scar where he'd had a rather unsuccessful encounter with a manacle.

"I don't know what possessed you," said Wicks.

"I dislike to be idle," said Gerald.

"Idle is what you're made for," muttered Wicks.

"It isn't," said Gerald. "You've not the slightest idea what I'm made for."

"You're not made for this," said Wicks. "Sailing. I was born and raised to sail, no matter how hard it is, no matter what difficulty I might face, because it runs in my veins, my bones. You've no such draw in your blood, Poole. It's blue as anything."

Demonstratively, Wicks pressed his thumb against one of the blue-purple lines of the veins that showed under Gerald's skin, at the inside of his elbow.

"You're meant to be better than the likes of us," said Wicks. "Sailors. You're meant to be satisfied with the life of leisure laid out for you. Almost nobody has the option to indulge it as you do."

This bothered Gerald for a reason he wasn't sure how to define, and he looked at Wicks' face, at how serious and concentrated it was. He kept on massaging Gerald's hands, thumbs pressing hard into the meat and soothing away the ache.

"I'm not better than anybody," said Gerald. "I don't want to be better than anybody. I just want to be left in peace is all."

"Labouring before the mast is your idea of peace, is it?" asked Wicks.

"It's natural to want to do something with one's hours. Wouldn't you go mad, sitting about with nothing to do all the time? Were you discharged out of the navy and told you couldn't work anywhere else, wouldn't you hate to be idle? *Ow*, Lieutenant, that hurts—!"

Wicks' grip on one of his fingers had suddenly become very tight, and Wicks now withdrew his hands, laying his palms flat against the table.

“Would I become a slut, you mean?” asked Wicks coldly.

“I don’t fuck men out of boredom,” said Gerald. “I do it because I like it, and it doesn’t harm anyone except me, if I ask for a pleasant harm.”

He reached up, touching the bruises Thwaites had left around his neck earlier. They were sore, but it was a pleasant soreness when he brushed his fingers over them, and Wicks looked at him in a very foul way.

“And what about God?” asked Wicks.

“What about Him? Last I checked, He’s never been in my bed.”

“You don’t think it’s a sin?” asked Wicks. “Man made in the image of God, and woman beside him, and you would set one aside?”

“By that logic, I’m less sinful than you are,” said Gerald. “Only wanting to fuck the image of God, and not wanting to fuck anything less.”

Wicks stared, and Thwaites, who had been walking past, laughed so hard that he wheezed as he went on.

“I want for men the same way I want for food and water,” said Gerald. “It’s not a sin to be hungry or thirsty or tired – it shouldn’t be a sin to want a fuck.”

Wicks took his arm back, sliding his thumbs up the length of Gerald’s arm, tracing his veins.

“Didn’t you want me?” asked Gerald quietly. “On the— On the Ambition, perhaps you didn’t want me then, but don’t you want me now?”

“My orders were to keep you well and healthy,” said Wicks. “Keep you from being hurt or distressed or offended. That last was made the most difficult, given that you kept throwing yourself in amongst the sailors, given how they talked about you as soon as you walked away.”

“They talked about me?” asked Gerald.

"Within your earshot at times, not that you noticed. Some of them figured you for a molly from the outset."

Gerald didn't know what to make of Wicks' expression, and he tilted his head slightly. "That bothered you?"

"You recall Robert Foyett's blackened eye?"

"I recall Robert Foyett. He was quite handsome."

"He called you a sodomite," said Wicks coldly.

"He wasn't wrong."

"And implied that I had been put in my position that I could service you."

Gerald turned his head away, curling up and then straightening his fingers, feeling how much easier they moved now, not so stiff. "I'm sorry for that," he said softly. "I had no idea you had punched another sailor to defend my honour."

"I had yet to learn you don't have any."

"I do," said Gerald. "I can show you, if you like – it's between my legs."

Wicks looked down, bowing his head, and although he seemed bashful, Gerald almost caught a glimpse of his strange, muted smile – an elusive thing, but very handsome.

"I didn't mean for you to fuck me," said Gerald. "Last night. I *was* cold – and what's more, you were cold as well. It just seemed foolish for us both to freeze."

"You won't be cold again," Wicks promised.

"I don't see what you have against me working. You stopped me on the Ambition and here, but you know I'm bound for work anyway, once I'm at home in Italy."

"I won't be responsible for you at that juncture," said Wicks.

"I don't want you to be responsible for me," said Gerald sharply. "Who asked you to be responsible for me?"

Wicks, slowly moving his jaw, said, "The way I see it, some men are made to toil, and others to manage that toil, and others still to sit by idle."

"I don't believe you," said Gerald. "I don't believe that you believe that."

"It's a natural truth of the world," said Wicks, although he didn't seem happy about it, his lips drawn into a deep frown. "It doesn't matter if we like it. It's just the way things are – a truth we're all made to live with. Just as men and women are meant for one another."

"Truth is a personal thing, I think," said Gerald. "I've yet to meet a truth of life that universally applies."

"Perhaps some truths are applied more rigorously to some people than others," said Wicks.

Gerald furrowed his brow, not knowing what to make of that, but he could see that Wicks seemed unhappy. He turned their hands around, stroking Wicks' wrists, his forearms, and Wicks closed his eyes a moment, exhaling.

Thwaites came up behind him, and just as Gerald loosely enclosed Wicks' wrists with his hands, not even remotely managing to enclose them wholly, Thwaites put his own hands on Gerald's shoulders, and put his fingers hard into the exhausted, stiff muscle he found there, making him groan sharply in mixed pain and pleasure.

"Ever had two men at once, Poole?" asked Thwaites as he pressed down in ways that made Gerald's flesh turn to jelly, making him gasp and moan, though he tried his best to keep it pitched low.

"Mm," Gerald hummed, and his cheeks flushed slightly red even before he saw the scandalised expression on Wicks' face.

“Interest you, that idea, Wicks?” asked Thwaites.

Wicks said nothing, but there was a new expression on his face that Gerald hadn’t seen from him before. His lips were parted, his eyes wide, and under the table, his knees brushed against Gerald’s as he pressed them tight together.

“Look at that,” said Thwaites softly. “It would seem I’ve found a cog.”

Part III

That night, Gerald slept against the barrel chest of Second Lieutenant Jack Wicks, and found that he let out such stupendous heat he might as well have been a furnace.

It was divine.

He was frustrated, somewhat – since he went to sea he'd scarcely had a moment truly alone to comb his hair, let alone bring himself off, and it seemed as though Thwaites got a good deal of pleasure from winding him up, only to delight in watching as he went absolutely nowhere at all.

Like this, it was worse, feeling the heat of Wicks' body, the rise and fall of his great chest, one of his hands underneath Gerald's shirt so as to rest on the small of his back, and as for what laid between Wicks' legs—

It was safe to say that his loose trousers bulged significantly with the morn.

Gerald had never been made to lie so very, tantalising close to something he couldn't partake in in all his life, and felt rather like Eve must have, if she'd been made to sleep in the damned tree with its fruit poking up against hers.

To his relief, once he was out of bed, Gerald was not made to sit in silence again: the next day he went about with Creed once more, and he saw that Wicks, too, was working, had fallen in amongst the sailors on the top deck.

He couldn't help but wonder if Wicks enjoyed the work as he did – if he enjoyed the ache in his bones that came after, if he enjoyed how the work occupied the whole busy thrill of his mind and shut everything else entirely out, so that he felt calm and focused and consumed with the rhythm of it. Or, did Wicks do it only because he felt it was what he had to do?

Thwaites wasn't making him work, and had told him several times that if it pleased him, he was welcome to sit aside with a book and read instead – had said, even, that if he wanted to keep a weather eye on Gerald, that he might do so above decks, or from the rigging.

Was he working only to watch Gerald? Did working help his mind quieten, let him relax where he couldn't before? Did he work because he felt it was fair, because Gerald was working – did he work because he felt it might help their chances? Because the work was there, and he couldn't concentrate on reading anyway?

Or because the work was sailing, and Wicks was a sailor to his core, and it was only right that he should sail, no matter the circumstances?

It was impossible to have any idea of how Wicks thought about anything, or what processes went on in his mind – he was not forthcoming with any of them, no matter how often or how much Gerald asked, or the manners in which he asked. Wicks wasn't forthcoming with anything at all.

The days passed in this manner.

It was not that Thwaites ceased to tease because he continued with aplomb: twice, he caught Gerald below decks and pinned him against the wall, kissed him as he slid his knee between Gerald's legs before pulling back, walking away, and leaving him heavy-breathing and faint.

Several times, he smacked Gerald's arse as he walked by, or greeted him by tugging his head back by the hair to kiss his neck or bite at his ear.

For all these casual movements at seduction, attempts to enter the captain's cabin were met with laughter and certain refusal, and no matter that Gerald flirted with other sailors on the Lamia, none of them would indulge him.

"I feel I am being tortured," he said over dinner one night.

"Darling thing, I've not even begun to torture you," said Thwaites, and squeezed his backside, but pulled his hand away when Gerald tried to lean into him. "Have you been torturing him, Wicks?"

"I've been sleeping," said Wicks plainly.

"All night?" asked Thwaites, arching one eyebrow.

"All night."

"Tut *tut*, Second Lieutenant."

Land showed the next day on the horizon, and Gerald stood at the edge of the deck and looked out as they approached.

Wicks, who had come up beside him, asked quietly, "What if your family doesn't pay the ransom?" and Gerald lashed out so suddenly he wasn't aware of what he was doing before his hand slapped against Wicks', making him lean back in surprise.

"What? How *dare* you! Of course they will!"

Wicks, faltering, looked out to sea, and said, "Seems convenient, that's all."

"Convenient?"

"If you're a— if you're a liability, I mean," said Wicks slowly. He spoke almost falteringly, as though he were careful to judge his words – and he didn't at all sound as though he were saying this with any cruel intent, which if anything, made it worse. "If they think you're liable to be tried for sodomy at any moment, and suddenly you die at sea, that's a big problem solved for the family's respectability."

Gerald was aware he had tears in his eyes, very suddenly overcome with a terrible fear indeed. It was not one that had occurred to him even for a moment, and on Wicks' face there was an expression of surprise, as though he expected Gerald not to be affected.

"Oh," he said, "Poole—"

"Up for a game of Whist, lads? We— Oh," said Cotton, when Gerald turned around.

"I don't know what you're all saying *oh* for," said Gerald fiercely, wiping so hard at his eyes he was liable to wake tomorrow with new bruises. "It's only salt water. You're surrounded by it all the livelong day!"

"What in Christ's name did you say to him?" Gerald heard Cotton ask as he walked furiously away.

Wicks' reply was too quiet to make out as he stormed in the direction of the stairs below deck, but he heard Cotton's response: "Jack, lad, you are stupid."

When Gerald fell over Thwaites' lap, Thwaites adjusted his chair, but kept on writing, one of his hands resting on Gerald's lower back as he continued to note his calculations in his diary.

"Aren't you going to ask me what's wrong?" asked Gerald in a miserable voice, aware of the vulnerable indignity of his position, straddling the captain's lap, his hands around his neck and face buried in his shoulder, the chair creaking under their combined weights.

With little interest, Thwaites asked, "Did Wicks say something quite blunt and tactless and seem surprised that it upset you?"

"Yes."

"I thought it might be something along those lines."

"You're just going to let me sit here?"

"The air is cooling as the night sets in," said Thwaites, neatly blotting his page. "Had you not arrived, I'd have called the ship's cat, and as well as being quite a bit smaller than you, she bites from time to time, and her arse isn't nearly so nice as your own."

"What about her whiskers?"

"Her whiskers? Posh, I think only of yours."

"Her tail?"

"Who needs one?"

"Her ears?"

"Ah, there you have me. Pagoda does have quite charming little ears. Let me see..." Thwaites dragged his teeth over the shell of Gerald's ear, making him shiver. "Hm, no, no," said the captain in mild tones. "I think yours do win out."

"Captain," said Gerald, "if my family don't pay the ransom, will you kill me?"

"You think they won't?"

"I thought they would. They always have before, every time, except for the occasions when I rendered a ransom unnecessary – it never occurred to me they wouldn't. But Wicks says it'd be very convenient for them if I died."

"I'm sure he didn't say it quite like that."

"But it's how he meant it."

"Hush," said Thwaites, and adjusted him. "I need to concentrate on my sums."

Gerald, disconsolate, fell half-asleep, and melted into the weight and muscle of Thwaites' chest.

* * *

Jack, powerless, stared after Poole as he stalked away, eyes streaming with tears. He didn't know what it was about Poole's tears that rendered him so powerless – he'd never known a man to cry so easily as Poole did, and didn't think he'd ever known a woman intimately enough that he should witness her crying.

It didn't seem that Poole did it on purpose, even, because every time he seemed so embarrassed.

"What in Christ's name did you say to him?" asked Cotton beside him.

In barely more than a murmur, Jack said, "I asked if perhaps his family wouldn't want him back. For the ransom, I mean."

Cotton sighed, shifting his arm almost as if he was going to reach up and pat Jack's arm, but he didn't. He just said, "Jack, lad, you are stupid. Come with me, now, help me set one of the new covers over the dinghy and we'll replace the one that's gotten ripped."

It was a relief to be occupied.

A ship was a ship was a ship, and no matter that he was amongst pirates, that he was amongst a crew unlike any navy or collection of merchantmen in the world, this philosophy carried even here upon the Lamia: the work remained the same, and occupied the mind as much as it did the body, allowed him to give himself over to something greater than himself and let the rhythm of the work to take him over.

It wasn't that he was made for the work – he had learned to become a sailor just as he had learned to become anything, and although he felt it was right he should sail, because his father sailed, because his father's father had sailed, and his father too, because it was in his blood, it wasn't what his blood was made of.

He sailed because there was nothing else he could do, should do – and even were it the case he had the desire for another position, who would give it to him? At least within the navy, his father's name counted for something, his father's influence – and he hated how he had to rely on it, despised how he had to count on his father's position in order to justify his own, but he needed *some* position for which to make a name, a reputation, for himself, and then—

And then. What powerless fucking words they were.

He'd never be an admiral, not like his father, wasn't foolish enough to believe it might be possible for him to attain that rank, and he didn't really allow himself to hope for command of his own ship, but he didn't *need* command.

He didn't yearn for command – command was difficult for any man to aspire to, because to command meant to understand one's men, not just in their individual persons, but in their intersections with one another, and those hundreds of combinations, how they acted as groups and tribes and collectives within the crew, and then there was the beast of the crew itself.

A crew could so easily turn against their captain, and if Jack ever managed to take a captaincy in the first place, if he ever managed to get a crew who respected him, who thought him worthy of his position, which would be near impossible, their respect of him would be like as not to turn upon a penny, and be lost almost as soon as it was gained, as soon as weather turned average, let alone poor, and the barest hardship was imagined.

It wasn't command he wanted.

He wasn't so arrogant or so stupid as to believe that even if he went to sea and single-handedly sunk every pirate ship along the Barbary Coast, sent the misbegotten profits of all these predatory crews back to the Royal Treasury, it would never overcome the fact of what he was in most men's eyes: Black-skinned and of *impure blood,* plainly an African heathen, no matter that he was as Christian as any of them, and had never left England until he'd joined the navy to serve the King.

But he didn't need command – all he needed was some renown, some bare renown to carry him through on the strength of his own deeds, and when he retired from naval service in ten years, in fifteen or twenty, they would serve enough to allow him enough to barter for a sense of privacy, or barest legitimacy.

He'd never live as his father did, as ignorant as his father was of the fact at times, but he could be *comfortable*, he thought. He would sail until he didn't have to any longer, until his deeds at sea would pay his way on land, and with all the pay he'd carefully saved, he would get lodgings for himself, position himself somewhere – he'd find a wife for himself, and he'd make use of his expertise in advising other sailors, maybe, or write some sort of memoir.

Wouldn't this business be tremendous fodder for that, if he only survived it?

"He's a stupid, self-centred lad," said Cotton, and Jack looked up from the canvas the two of them had been unfolding, watching the other man. Cotton and Thwaites, Cotton had mentioned to him, were really quite alike in age, but Cotton looked the senior of the two of them.

Where Thwaites, tall and handsome, was only showing the most dignified beginnings of silver at his temples, and a few shining silver strands amidst the beautiful sheen of his black hair, his brown skin smooth and barely marked by sun or age, only by the occasional nick of the sword or a tattooist's needle, Cotton wore his age in the beleaguered and resigned way many men wore their clothes.

He was creased and sun-stained, the colour in his hair no longer to be relied upon – Cotton himself had had dark hair, once upon a time, a sort of chestnut brown, Jack wouldn't wager, but now it was turning to grey in great patches, and his beard was marked with dozens of shades of colour. Even with how ever many years he'd served sailing, his skin was not especially brown: his skin was naturally pale, and tended to turn red instead of bronzing, although it seemed the man didn't much burn.

"He's rich," said Jack. "And air-headed. His like is ten a penny. If we started prosecuting them, there'd not be a gaol with any space left."

Cotton laughed, shaking out the canvas piece and taking up a rope to fasten it in place. "Wasn't suggesting we put him before a court, though there's men who'd do that to fools like him. I was saying it because he doesn't know what the fuck you're at with him – doesn't know what the fuck people are at with himself, even."

"You think me disloyal, I suppose," said Jack, uncertain, and Cotton laughed at that, too, tipping back his head, and then he shook it. Thwaites' eyes were hypnotising, hazel in a way that caught the light, showing flecks of green and gold when he was in the sun, but Cotton's eyes in their own way were striking – although he had darker hair, his eyes were lighter, a shining blue that looked all the bluer for how red his cheeks tended to be.

"The fuck do you have to be loyal to?" he asked. "Wait, wait, I know," he said, putting up his hand when Jack opened his mouth, "they told you to look after him, I know, but that's not what I mean. You two barely fucking know one another. Am I right?"

"What purpose does this interview serve?" asked Jack.

"Interview," said Cotton, shaking his head and chuckling to himself. "Purpose. God save me from lads with educations."

"You'd rather I not be educated, sir?" asked Jack coolly.

"Have all the education you like, just keep it to yourself," said Cotton, and Jack, surprised despite himself, huffed out a sound he didn't want to admit was a laugh, and Cotton grinned at him. "What I'm trying to say to you is that it's *not* just that he's rich. Oh, he's rich, yes, privileged little cunt raised to sit on his arse and manage other people rushing about, and pale as milk for all that, a delicate little white Englishman."

Jack didn't let himself frown, didn't let himself react, but he did look at Cotton askance, not quite sure what to make of the way he was talking, what was coming of it.

Cotton saw him looking, and said, "Yeah, I know. Ship like this, comes to be you notice the differences a man's colour makes with how people treat him, and how different they treat you. Many's a time we have to think of strategy when it comes to selling our gear on – see if we send someone a merchant thinks he can take advantage of, someone he wants to try to undercut, or a white man if he feels alone with no other whites around, wants to feel superior. Ced's a master of knowing who'll suit best, use it to our favour."

"Criminals are criminals," said Jack. "I would have thought they'd be happiest with their own, no matter what colour their criminal companions."

"Crime, aye," said Cotton. "We steal bales of silk from some fuck merchant, and there's crime – a navy steals a man, decides he should be made to slave away, and there's the law."

"Am I not labouring at your behest this moment, Mr Cotton?"

"Is there not a promise of freedom, when your ransom is paid?" was the easy reply, and there was something mocking in Cotton's fake accent, like he was mimicking Thwaites. "How many men taken get that luxury?"

Jack was silent a second, the two of them working together, passing the rope back and forth in neat, criss-crossing motions. "It's not a just world, Mr Cotton," said Jack. "And none of us can make it so – the best we can do is survive."

"It's not a just world," Cotton agreed. "Your lad don't know that, you know. He's... simple. You get that, don't you? You understand that?"

Jack blinked, not sure what to make of that at all, and he frowned slightly at Cotton, at his blunt tone, his plain expression. Cotton sighed, chuckling, as he kept at his work, and said, "S'not any failing on the lad's part, well, I don't think, anyway. He reminds me of Ced, when the two of us were that age – you can control yourself, discipline yourself. He can't. He's like a ship with full sails but no command of his rudder – goes right fast, when the winds are good, but when they're not, loses control and comes apart. Wind at the wrong angle, when he can't turn his way around, are liable to rip his ropes from their moorings, send him keeling over as fast as he can blink. And he's simple, in the head." Cotton tapped the sides of his temple. "Understands only what you say, what you mean underneath, that's a fucking mystery to him. You want him to understand what you mean to say to him, you have to say it. I know it's not very English, but anything but frank speaking will have you at a loss with him."

"I feel Mr Poole's faculties are not quite as defective as you make out," said Jack sceptically, and Cotton grinned to himself, passing the other side of the rope over to Jack so that they could pass it between them to lash the canvas down.

"He's not defective," said Cotton, softer now, with a fond smile pulling at his mouth – thinking of Thwaites, no doubt, and not Poole. "But he'll cry like that, from time to time, over what seems like fucking nothing – and it will be nothing, 'cept he'll overflow with it."

"You mean to tell me your Captain Thwaites cries behind closed doors?" asked Jack.

"If only," said Cotton. "It's the best I can do when *he* overflows to keep him from setting fires."

Jack sniggered, and he cut it short, pressing his lips tight together, clenching his jaw, trying to raise his head and be dignified. Cotton, still smiling, kept on working the rope between their hands.

"Not saying it to excuse him when he drives you doolally," said Cotton. "Don't mean you shouldn't tell him when he's wrong – if anything, you should do it more, state it plainly. But you just think of him flouncing us all at cards, and taking it for granted that we were all making up calculations, same as him."

"Again, I have to question what prompts you to give me this advice," said Jack. "From the goodness of your heart?"

"Ain't no good in my heart," said Cotton. "But the thing about birds, lad, is they can recognise when they're of a feather."

"And how similar in hue our feathers are," remarked Jack, making Cotton chuckle, but he didn't flinch away or draw himself back, didn't even seem surprised.

"Not pretending to know how you've got it, or have experienced anything like it," said Cotton. "Even men the same colour as me, lads like Poole, I wouldn't pretend to know how he's lived his life or how it's run over him. But he don't play by the rules, see, that's his problem – even when he sees the rules unspoken, which is no guarantee, he can't control himself enough to follow them. He gets overwhelmed or overexcited or over some man's handsome face, and then he does as he does, and doesn't even realise he's done wrong until after he's flogged for it."

"He's never been flogged," said Jack, and Cotton snorted.

"You're a fucking literal one, I'll give you that," he said. "The two of you are fine matched."

Jack pressed his lips tight together. He wanted to say that he wasn't like Poole, wasn't like Thwaites, that he wasn't *like that*, but would that hurt their chances of survival? Was it the case that they'd only been allowed to live so far because Thwaites and Cotton, with whatever strange perversion of marriage they had toward one another, saw themselves in what Jack and Poole were feigning – what Jack had been trying to feign?

Not that it mattered, he supposed.

Poole was already abandoning it in favour of begging Thwaites for any attention he could, and a part of that grated although he ought be grateful in a way. Jack thought of the way Poole slept with him in the bed, the way he crammed his body against Jack's as though he were some cat or rabbit, certain he would freeze to death and desperate to leech any warmth he could, and yet there was something so peaceful in it, so impossibly enticing.

Times were that once or twice, in moments of quiet today, that Wicks had wondered distantly what it might be like to go on like this forever, to feel Poole's weight on top of his chest, his arms wrapped around Jack's body, his heart beating steadily, his breathing even, making soft sounds in his sleep.

There was something precious in it, and yet more than that, there was something protective in it – it was a ridiculous thought, that Poole might protect him from a mosquito, let alone a real threat, and yet with Poole as his blanket, he almost felt safer than he ever had before, as though there were something right in the world he'd never considered before might be wrong.

It was stupid, of course.

This was stolen time, and they were stolen men, and if they made it out of all this alive, it was possible Wicks' life would be stolen too.

He kept oscillating, he knew, between wild hope and what he felt might be optimism and cynical certainty that all was already lost, and he hated that he didn't know which instinct he ought trust, because there had never been consistency in what the universe had thrown at him thus far, except that he should suffer for things he was, rather than things he'd done.

"When you asked him if his family'd pay ransom," said Cotton, tying off the boat, "and said it'd be better for them to let him go? I bet you were wondering about his family, right? I bet you were thinking – and rightly – about what rich cunts like them are like, thinking of things in terms of money, willing to fuck over anybody alive, so long as more money comes of it."

Jack didn't say anything.

"What he heard," went on Cotton, leaning back on his heels, "is that you think he isn't worth paying for."

"That's not what I told him," said Jack. "That's not... that's not even remotely what I said."

"I know," said Cotton. "And I bet no one ever told him people play cards by working out the odds so precise in their heads neither, but it's what he thought was the case – just like he thinks every other man wants to fuck him, or would fuck him if they had the chance, because he's not been proved wrong, just like it hasn't occurred to him a lot of men would do him harm just because it suited them, for no reason at all, 'cause that's not how he thinks. He's naive, for certain, and simple, as I told you. How do I explain it?" The older man sighed, putting his hands on his hips and looking out over the bow, out to the blue skies, the land that was growing closer and closer on the horizon. "Thwaites and Poole, they see the world the way you or I'd see it through a telescope. Up close, and they see the details we don't, but they miss a lot of the stuff outside it – and it doesn't occur to them that we should see things any differently than they do, unless they're specifically reminded."

"That's ridiculous," said Jack, and Cotton laughed the hardest yet at that.

"Aye, lad, *they're* ridiculous," he said, gearing up to walk away. "Or haven't you noticed?"

That night, Jack stirred in the middle of the night to the sound of Poole's voice, and he blinked in the gloom as Poole said again, his voice soft and small, his chin resting on the cushioned flesh over Jack's sternum, "Jack? Are you awake?"

"What?" asked Jack.

"Would you pay a ransom?" asked Poole. "If someone kidnapped me from you?"

He was half-asleep, and half-certain he was dreaming as he turned them over, lying on his side and pulling Poole up against him, burying his nose into the softness of Poole's hair. His mouth moved without his permission, and he wanted to regret it, but he was asleep too quickly again to remember to do so.

"I'd pay the world for you," Jack mumbled sleepily, and Poole curled closer into his chest.

* * *

The ship was brought into some hidden bay, miles and miles away, it seemed to Gerald Poole, from almost anywhere, where there was a secreted little dock and the Lamia's sails were quite obscured unless someone actually followed them inside.

There were caves here, dozens upon dozens of them, and Gerald watched as some of their cargo was secreted within, parted and parcelled and set into hidden shelves and alcoves, covered over with netting, as Thwaites oversaw this unloading with Cotton, and made notations upon a board.

Gerald had been ushered out of the way when he'd tried to assist in unloading things, had been told he was too small and to get out of the way, but somehow it hadn't felt unkind, as it sometimes felt when he was being bothersome – he preferred to be told frankly than not be told at all, and Creed had gotten hold of him and bid him come back up the gangplank – which Gerald now walked with ease – to help the cook scale fish for supper.

Gerald was untroubled by this work, liked its rhythm and its complexity, and he laughed with delight when one of the sailors brought in two octopus that they'd trapped in the rocks, and the cook had shown him how to piece them apart and remove their beaks.

Later in the afternoon, when the sun was still warm but beginning its descent, they ate their dinner upon the shore, and many of the sailors were sitting all across the beach or up under the trees further up from the sand.

In the warm, shallow water of a small natural pool, the captain reclined naked, and Gerald, who had not bathed in warm water for what felt like centuries, had stripped off to join him. The pool was empty of small creatures, but for some limpets and a slimy algae that smoothed out the few rough edges of the sea-washed rock under their backs, but the nearby pools were not.

The smaller ones were awash with life, and Gerald laid alongside the captain, watching little fish and crabs hop between the smaller pools beside them. It was fascinating, the way they moved, the darting little ways the fish jumped between algaes and one another, startling each other, and when he watched one of the crabs, it sat back and very calmly snipped off the tiniest pieces of algae with its little pincers, like a gardener pursuing topiary, except that as far as Gerald knew, gardeners didn't regularly put their offcuts between their mandibles and devour them once snipped away.

"Is that a shark bite?" asked Wicks, and Gerald looked up at him.

Wicks, standing at the foot of the pool Gerald and Thwaites were lying back in, was of course still fully clothed, although he had deigned to remove his jacket, so that Gerald could see the way the powerful muscles of his arms and the weight of his chest threatened to burst out of the shirt.

Cotton was sitting at the edge of the pool, and although he didn't get in with them, nor take off his clothes as Thwaites had, he had rolled up his trousers and his feet rested in the water with waters lapping up to his ankles. His feet and Thwaites regularly touched against one another, and Gerald felt a sense of distant jealousy at the casual intimacy of it, although he and Thwaites rested both of them nude and shoulder to shoulder.

The thought occurred to him that it perhaps wasn't Cotton precisely that he was jealous of, but the connection he shared with Thwaites.

Wicks, of course, was scowling with disapproval down at Thwaites and Gerald both, but now and then his gaze would flit over their bodies, as if he was pretending not to do it. Thwaites' leg had lifted out of the water, and Gerald looked at the bitten circle of toothy marks there. The mouth that had bitten him had been too large to leave a complete ring, and the individual bites showed that the teeth had been quite large indeed.

"Ah," said Thwaites, gesturing dismissively with one handsome hand. "Yes. It's not an interesting story."

"It's fucking funny though," said Cotton.

"Haven't you inventory still to oversee?" Thwaites asked coldly.

"I'm overseeing it right now," said Cotton. "It's paddling in a pool and bothering a hermit crab."

Gerald gently put the crab back.

"The captain, as I'm sure you've observed," said Cotton to Wicks, putting on a funny, more clipped and cultivated voice that Gerald could distantly recognise as modelled on Thwaites' own, "is a man who would set a fire just to see what it burned."

"I have observed this, yes," said Wicks cleanly, in a voice like Gerald's, and Gerald wrinkled his nose.

"He is curious beyond sense or reason."

"This matches with my estimates of his character thus far."

"He is a voyeur, a tease, and a machinator of all manner of oddities."

"I see the defendant," said Wicks, "and find him guilty on all three counts."

Gerald stifled his giggle when he saw Wicks' mouth twitch, because he was trying not to smile, and Thwaites looked at him from the side before crossing his arms over his handsome, naked chest and looking between Cotton and Wicks. "Are you two quite finished?"

"If you'd like to tell the story, Captain," said Cotton innocently, spreading his hands, "be my guest."

"Who has need of a story?" said Thwaites. As well as Thwaites' tattoos of constellations, and a few others that Gerald had come to regard as staples amongst sailors – over one thigh, a mermaid that shimmied when he bent the joint of his knee, and over his chest, skulls and crossbones and maps and gemstones – he had two sharks banding the top of his upper arm. When he moved his arm now, gesturing once more, the sharks moved as though the muscle were their water, and it made him smile. "It is as simple as that I like sharks."

"So you let one bite you?" asked Gerald.

"Why not?" was Thwaites' retort, keeping his gaze. "It's how you show you like men."

Cotton, smirking, said, "Captain—"

"Yes, yes, Mr Cotton," grumbled Thwaites, leaning back with the sun-warmed water washing over his skin. Sighing, he folded his hands over the flat of his belly. "We were all young once," said he. "And with youth comes foolishness and foolhardiness. When I was but a stripling youth, somewhat younger than Poole here..." He trailed off a moment, and his glittering eyes, dark pools all full of emeralds and gold, looked to Gerald, to Wicks, and then to Cotton again. "Paul," he said. "Do you really think—"

"I do," said Cotton firmly.

“It was my first long voyage at sea,” said Thwaites. “I was not yet anointed with blood to this vilest of arts, the art of piracy: I was with a merchant vessel, like my father before me. I had been educated, of course, and schooled very keenly, but even the keenest of educations does not prepare one for what comes after. Ever did I marvel at the wonders I saw upon the oceans.

“We came upon, of all things, the great carcass of a sperm whale – it was too old to be of much use, and all its oil had mostly spread out in the water in a rainbow sheen. It smelled quite awful, and made a few boys ill. But upon a whale so great as this one supped some great sea creatures.”

“Great indeed,” intoned Cotton, and Thwaites splashed water at him, making him laugh.

“Your father vouched for you to go to sea?” asked Wicks.

“He did, but my father was not well-liked,” said Thwaites, his voice very casual and easy. “He was corrupt, but not intelligent – it is a fine thing to be corruptible, but if one is too stupid to carry it off, he is bound for a life of quotidian insignificance if he is lucky, and death by murder or his own clumsiness if he is not. I found my way onto this particular ship by bartering and blackmailing my way aboard. I was as well-treated as any of the darling petty officers, and seeing how well-treated I was, they naturally assumed I was some manner of secret prince or otherwise. I used that assumption quite carefully going on – there’s some about who still think me an undisclosed Yuvaraja, in line for a foreign throne.”

“That’s treacherous,” said Wicks.

“So too are the seas, darling man,” said Thwaites. “Do you scorn them for their nature as well?”

“Blackmailing your way through ships and sailing life,” said Wicks, “yes, perhaps I would.”

"Why shouldn't I have taken what I wanted, when I found it was so easy to grasp hold of, and take? Those stupid men would have mistreated me, believing themselves superior because they had their English blood and their white skin, where I had half of one and none of the other – you think me wrong for disproving their prejudice? Did I not simply outplay them at their game, without letting on that I knew their rules?"

Wicks curled his lip, and gave Thwaites such a foul look that Gerald shivered. "Your mother taught you this?"

"My mother taught me poetry and song," said Thwaites softly. "She taught me beauty, and grace, and how to treat others – taught me so well, in fact, that I command all these fine gentlemen, not a *gentleman* among them, and know how to treat them well, that each of them feels respected and a part of this crew, as well he should. It was my father who taught me treachery – having better brains than he did, I simply improved on his technique."

Having been growing impatient for some few moments, Gerald said a little louder than he intended to, "The *whale*, Captain."

Thwaites laughed, and curled his fingers in Gerald's hair, and Wicks stiffened, looking down at him with his mouth twisted. "Oh, I'm *sorry*, darling, are you bored? Yes, the whale. We had to lay anchor anyway, so we stopped a while, and I spent some time observing the carcass, the fish that came to nip at it, and the birds that swooped down to perch atop it before they would fly away. And the sharks, too."

"Sharks?" repeated Gerald, delighted.

"Oh, yes."

"Of course there'd be sharks," said Wicks irritably. "He's got a bite from a shark. It wasn't going to be a squid, was it?"

Gerald tossed a handful of seaweed at him, which Wicks deftly sidestepped.

"Most of them," said Thwaites placatingly, "were smaller things. Sharks from the reef below, dog fish, nothing impressive, not at first. But then... Then, a great shadow moved in the water, some three times the length of me easily – a white shark, a lamia, a beast of the oceans deep. Her fin jutted from the water, and in rising, she parted the waves."

"Like Moses," offered Gerald.

"Exactly like Moses," agreed Thwaites. They both laughed, Cotton too, when Wicks rolled his eyes.

"I was fascinated with the creature," said Thwaites. "She was the first to arrive, having smelt out the whale in the water, and I sketched her a few times, and kept peering down at her to see her black eyes, the roundness of her snout coming down to the point of her mouth, the shape of her fins, her huge tail. I had only ever, before now, seen them harpooned or half-gutted. I never realised before that moment how *quickly* they moved in the water, nor really grasped how they moved. That great tail of hers moved from side to side to propel her through the brine – have you ever seen a man use a rope saw to fell a tree?"

Thwaites made movements with his hands, putting out one hand before he drew it back and pushed forward with the other, completing this motion several times. "That is the motion of their tails, the shark's, a great push and pull. So delighted was I by the very sight that I... Well."

Thwaites stopped, and Cotton began – that was their nature by now, Gerald supposed.

"I," said Cotton, "was a rigger on this same vessel. So when one of the fancy petty officers comes to me, little rich prick in his fancy coat who's only just learning the sea, and says, "Mr Cotton, I'm going up the rigging, don't you mind me," I says, "Yes, sir, as you like, sir," and think nothing of it."

Thwaites chuckled, looking sheepish and strangely bashful in a way that made Gerald's chest feel warm and full.

"How old are you?" asked Gerald curiously of Cotton, who frowned at him.

"Never you fucking mind."

"Older than Captain Thwaites."

"By three years," said Cotton. "I'm no octogenarian."

"Oh," said Gerald, frowning and looking at Cotton with renewed interest. "I didn't realise you were so close in age. You *look*—" Thwaites laid a hand on Gerald's chest and looked at him meaningfully, and somewhat lamely, Gerald amended his sentence to finish it with, "—very well for it, I'm sure."

Cotton worked his jaw a moment, his hands on his knees, and then looked to Thwaites. "May I kill him, Ced?"

"You may not," said Thwaites. "You may whip him, if you like, but I expect he'd like it too."

"Like as not I would," agreed Gerald.

"So," said Wicks, clearing his throat, "you were in the rigging."

"That I was," Thwaites agreed. "You see, with the whale so large as it was, I couldn't always see the shark, turning over and over the corpse as she was to bite at the best bits, and with all the whale's oil in the water, it was difficult to get a good look without the sun's shine above reflecting everything. I wanted a better look."

"Into the jaws of death," said Wicks dryly.

"Into the jaws of nature and her mysteries," corrected Thwaites in a prim voice, and Gerald laughed.

"The whale being on our starboard side, I climbed up the net and shimmied along the stays – I sort of leaned against the sheet of one of the mail sail, just over the clew. I'd shimmied along to rest over the mast tip where it stretched out over there – quite safe and secure I was, and from there, I had a bird's eye view of both shark and her meal."

"Until you fell," said Wicks.

"Until I fell," said Thwaites. "A sudden shift in the wind hit the sail at an odd angle, so that a corner of the sheet was caught by the wind and slapped me in the face – with the ship anchored, we only turned a bit, but it caught me off my balance. I pitched, caught enough of a grip on the stay a moment to cry for help, and fell."

"Into the water?" asked Gerald.

"Onto the whale, first," said Cotton. "Made a sort of rubbery splat."

"It was quite unpleasant," said Thwaites. "I don't know how whaler men do it – and they get *inside* the things to scrape out their brains, not just stand on top. Anyway, I tried to keep my balance upon the corpse, but it was unbalanced and unsteady."

"You managed it a while," said Cotton. "A few minutes at least you kept your balance, because we were nearly ready with a ring and rope."

"It didn't feel like long," Thwaites said. "In any case, the whale shifted beneath me and I slipped back into the oil-filmed brine."

"Quite a splash he made, too."

"Yes, thank you, Paul. I, of course, was quite terrified, and didn't know whether to splash about or what – I'd no idea where the shark was, and with all the oil in the water I couldn't even dip my head to look. I can't even describe to you the intensity of the stench, no doubt made all the more powerful by the fact that my eyes were closed. I heard the splash as they threw the ring into the water, and blindly, I swam.

"I don't know how fast I went, but it was as fast as I knew how, and just as I was about to grab the ring, my fingers brushing it, I felt this great, wrenching tear on the back of my leg as I was pulled under. It took me by such surprise that I screamed, gasping in sea water and spermaceti, a combination no man desires in his mouth or his lungs, I can assure you."

"He pulled you under?" Wicks asked, aghast.

"That she did," said Thwaites. "The pain in my leg was impossible, so much so that I thought she surely must have taken the whole thing with her, but she let me go a moment later and I rushed for the ring to be pulled aboard."

"But didn't your blood in the water send all the sharks there into a frenzy, all of them eager for a taste of man?" asked Gerald.

"Perhaps not all sharks share your proclivities," said Wicks, and this time when Gerald threw it, the seaweed hit him in the thigh.

"I don't believe so," said Thwaites. "Seems to me our lamia took a bite of me to see how I tasted, and found whale blubber to be a choicer meal – she didn't even take much flesh off me really, only what clung to her teeth. You can see from the scarring that there's not a great chunk missing, far less than you might expect. If I had fins, I'd use my mouth to look at things too, I bet."

"You don't have fins, and you do do that," said Cotton. "A fine picture you looked too, doused in sperm oil and sea water, coughing it up, bleeding all down your leg, and all you could say was how rough she felt when she came past you in the water."

"Such a rough skin," said Thwaites, his gaze far away in the memory, his tone marvelling. "So roughly textured I thought it might pull the skin off my palm, and all the *power* under that flesh too... I expect they'd be excellent to ride, sharks, if you could only convince them of the thing."

"We washed him off and the surgeon had a look at his leg," said Cotton when Thwaites trailed off again, looking wistful and dreamy. "He said he'd been very lucky our white pointer had such a pleasant meal in front of her, and that he posed so little interest. And he was whipped for it."

"For being bitten?" asked Gerald, and Cotton scoffed.

"For dangling from the mast like an idiot and falling in."

Thwaites chuckled regretfully, reaching down and idly brushing his fingers over the scarred flesh. "I'd do it again," he said. "She was quite gentle, really."

"You are mad," pronounced Wicks.

"I'd like to see a shark that big," said Gerald.

* * *

They sailed onwards, soon enough, and for all the work was pleasing, Gerald found he was overcome with anxiety. It distracted him from all his waking hours and interrupted his sleeping hours too, so that he frequently rolled out of bed with Wicks or woke up to Wicks irritably patting him for him to be quiet and still.

He struggled to imagine it, and yet for Wicks to say it so confidently, it had to be done all the time. Wicks was a sailor some years his senior, after all, a man of the world – he knew better than Gerald what the world was like.

His father *had* been furious about the most recent occasion, the second time in as many months he'd been pulled aside from some improper place and rushed aside before anyone might burst in to make some arrest. Gerald had never been before a magistrate, had been spared that humiliation thus far, but his father had seemed quite intent on the idea that he would be soon if he carried on.

How the man had snapped at him, how he'd *shouted*, but—

But his family were better than most, he thought.

He was the second youngest of four children, and not once had his father suggested he should get married if he didn't want to, and nor had any of his brothers pushed the thought, either, and no one had ever threatened him, or said anything unkind to him or very cruel, not family members.

And his aunt, she was a nice old woman, really, who couldn't care less that he should be in a nice house she owned if he wanted it, and his family *weren't* like most people's families, *weren't* like most people.

And he didn't think most people, didn't think anyone, would, but of all people, his family, they wouldn't just... They wouldn't, would they? Just let him die?

"My father," said Thwaites beside him where Gerald was looking out over the bow, making him jump, "tried to kill me."

"Really?" asked Gerald in a small voice, not bothering to ask how Thwaites had read his mind.

"Oh, yes," said Thwaites. "He tried to run me through with a blade, and then a poker."

"Why?"

Thwaites offered his cigarillo to Gerald, who shook his head, before he took a drag, blew out some smoke, and tapped the ash over the side.

"I tried to kill him first," he said. "Some words of anger passed between him and my mother, and he went to beat her over it. I saw red, wouldn't stand for that. If he'd hit her before, it had never been in my presence. I was ready to tear him limb from limb."

"You killed him, then?"

"Yes, but not that year," said Thwaites. "I was only twenty-eight, that year – I killed him three years back, the month before my fortieth birthday."

"Because he beat your mother?"

"Mm, no, no, of course not. My mother had long since left him by then and gone back to Madras, I sailed her and my sister home myself. She remarried, actually, her husband is a librarian or an accountant or a bookbinder or something, extremely dull man, but she seems to like him very much. No, I'd gone to visit for something or other, just to check he was alive, and he went to kick the dog. I wanted to ensure he didn't remarry – I didn't think there was a huge risk, but you know."

Gerald thought about this a moment, and then asked, "Is the dog still alive?"

"I think so. She was only a puppy, some sort of sheep dog thing. I gave her to the local smith. Very cute it was, too, sitting in that room, lit by the forge, and she sat on top of one of the cold anvils, sort of perched there, and tilted her head almost all the way around as she watched him shoe a horse." Thwaites tapped his fingers against the side's edge. He had waves tattooed on the backs of his knuckles, Gerald saw amongst the rings, and when he tapped his fingers, it was like they were swelling and moving. "It was a fine day, and very hot in the forge, as you would expect, but I felt cold to my bones. I really hadn't wanted to kill him, and I'd like to say I did it in a rash of anger, but it really wasn't that. I knew what I was doing, and did it with cold calculation, because I didn't want him to harm anybody more than he already had. He'd done more than his fair share of damage to those who didn't deserve it."

Thwaites did not sound especially sad as he said it, only thoughtful, speaking with a sort of distance that Gerald knew he could be capable of, at times – the sort of distance that got him told off, and told he was being monstrous over, even when it barely even mattered.

But then, Gerald had never killed a man, let alone his own father – he couldn't imagine doing such a thing in all his wildest nightmares.

"I sat there for quite some time," said Thwaites. "Waiting for the smith to finish his work, watching him shoe the horse, same as the dog. His name's Robin, the smith, and when I was a little boy I used to do the same thing, sit and just watch him work. He used to say he wished his sons would show the same interest, until he realised I had no interest in actually picking up the hammer and tongs, just that I liked to observe their workings. He helped me bury my father, and I left that town for the last time. Nothing tethers me to England any longer, my father dead, my mother, my brother, my sister, all departed, and Paul's family live in Oslo."

"He doesn't look Norwegian."

"According to you," said Thwaites, "he barely looks alive."

Gerald chuckled.

"He isn't, but his sister married a Norwegian, and when she went over to Norway, their father went with them."

Gerald nodded, and then looked down at the way the ship cut through the water, making it white and streaked by the separation. They were like a shark, he thought, but in reverse, cutting from above instead of below.

"Do you think I'm handsome?" he asked.

"I do," said Thwaites. "When certain stars are in alignment I plan to fuck you within an inch of your life."

"Not tonight?"

"Not tonight."

"Lots of men think I'm handsome," said Gerald. "I don't see why there has to be such secrecy and reticence about it. The way I see it, I'm very good-looking, and witty, and quite up for it, and the men I take up with are up for it too – I'd never try to trick a man into fucking me that didn't want to, nor force the matter even if I had the strength. Seems like half the men who'd hang me for it are just jealous they can't fuck me themselves, but they *could*, if they weren't such cowards."

"Not all the world's bigotries, young man, revolve around the enticement of your cock and finely-fleshed thighs, but I am sure your assumption applies to a not insignificant portion of them."

Gerald reached up for the cigarillo, taking it gently from Thwaites' hand, and took a puff.

"Still want to pick olives?" asked Thwaites.

"Yes, I'd like to try," said Gerald. "I hear you take a great big sheet and beat the trees, and all the olives fall into the sheet, and it makes a big racket, and all the cicadas sing."

"They don't sing," said Thwaites. "It's a sort of rattling scream."

"Oh," said Gerald, and handed the cigarillo back. "What now?"

"We sell our goods first, and then we make for a little island east of Sicily, in the middle of the Ionian Sea."

Gerald frowned. "In the Heptanese?"

"Not that far east," said Thwaites. "When I said in the middle, I rather meant in the middle. It's not an island, I'd wager, that you'll find on any of your maps – Paul has a knack for finding these undiscovered places. Don't worry, we'll send your family very accurate coordinates, that they not get lost."

Gerald nodded his head slowly, feeling a sort of grim and uncertain terror settle like a tree taking root in the pit of his stomach. He wondered if the tree would grow out of him, and break his ribs from the inside, and make him burst.

It felt like it might.

"You could have run away, you know," pointed out Thwaites in a soft voice like spun silk. "At our last port – you and Wicks both."

"Oh," said Gerald softly. "That hadn't occurred to me."

"Come," said Thwaites, and put his hand on Gerald's back, guiding him to follow. "Let's play a game of Whist."

Part IV

They traded some ways east of Tripoli, and it didn't occur to Gerald really, seriously, that neither of them had tried to escape until they were already sailing north again. He thought about asking Wicks about it, ask why he hadn't even suggested it, assuming he had thought of it where Gerald hadn't, but the matter wasn't currently foremost in Gerald's mind.

"You could come with me," he said, and Wicks glanced at him.

"What?"

It was late in the evening, and Gerald was sitting up and not reading his book, his legs entangled with Wicks' on the bed. Wicks' legs were very warm.

"To my aunt's house," said Gerald. "To pick olives. If you can't go back to sea, if the navy won't take you back."

"Oh," said Wicks quietly. He shifted his position on the pillow, curling his face more into Gerald's side, his blunt nose tickling at him, his breathing hot. It should have bothered him, really, but it didn't, not at all. He liked Wicks' head beside him on the pillow, Wicks' arm around his thighs, even though he couldn't see Wicks' face, the expression on it. "Poole, I like the sea," he murmured tiredly. "It's my place, a ship's deck."

"You talk an awful lot about people's *place*, as though it should matter."

"For some of us, Poole, it *does* matter. Not everyone has the luxury of setting aside the destiny strangers assign to us."

"Why, because you're not rich?"

Wicks sighed, hard, and he leaned back from Gerald's thigh, looking up at him. "Poole," he said. "You do see the differences between us, don't you? The differences between my hair and yours, my nose and yours, my *skin* and yours?"

"But you're English," said Gerald. "As English as I am. It's not as though people ought see you as anything less than I am."

"You think the average sailor doesn't look at me and see a man not so dissimilar to the man on the market block?"

"It's not as if *Britain's* made slavery legal, and we don't recognise slavery abroad – you've the same rights as I do, and should. Even escaped slaves have more rights in England than elsewhere - Lord Mansfield blocked them from sending that slave back to Jamaica once he reached the asylum of Britain's shores."

"James Somerset," muttered Wicks.

"My father's an abolitionist," said Gerald, "and he wrote an essay about—"

"Good for him," said Wicks loudly, sharply, and Gerald shut his mouth, seeing Wicks' frustration and not understanding what he was meant to do to assuage it, what he was meant to *say*, when Wicks wasn't a slave, had no relation to slaves, and had been in the navy – that *meant* he was his own man, didn't it? No matter the colour of his skin, he was a sailor as any other man.

"What about me?" asked Gerald lowly. "Where do you think my place is?"

"For now, I think right here will do," said Wicks, and pressed an infuriatingly lovely, painfully chaste kiss to Gerald's hip. His eyes were closed, and he seemed on the verge of returning to sleep.

Gerald, upset for reasons he couldn't hope to put into words, set his book aside and blew out the light.

* * *

Jack had excused himself from the table down on the sand, where they were roasting two goats over a fire, and he stood on the top of the hill, resting his elbows on an old section of wall. The island was a strange one, not one that he'd ever seen charted, and it didn't make sense in his head, where they were – but they were undeniably on land.

"I wondered where you were," said Thwaites in mild tones as he came up the last of the steps, and Jack glanced back at him. He was stripped down to his shirtsleeves with them rolled up to his elbows, and his vest and shirt were both worn open, such that he could see huge sections of his skin. There were tattoos on him, of course – the Argo on the back of his neck, the Pisces constellation over his heart, and more and more tattoos than that, a few dozen of them.

His hair was tied up in a loose and messy bun, a few strands free and falling around his shoulders, and it framed the handsome lines of his face; in the warmth and brightness of the sunlight, Wicks could see the star-like glitter of the honeydrops in his eyes.

"Your hair's getting a little longer," said Thwaites when Jack said nothing. "I'm told you're nearly out of that awful pomade, thank God – you needn't dread your hair if you don't like, but if you don't want it cutting, I'm sure one of the others can help you work. Creed's a dab hand with braiding, even for short hair, or he could at least do some twists for you."

Jack set his jaw, pressing his lips tightly together and pushing his palms firmer against the stone underneath him. "I need to pomade it," he said quietly. "Or it gets tangled."

"Do you comb it?"

"I can't get a comb through it *unless* I pomade it," said Jack irritably, and Thwaites smiled at him as he came to stand at his side, and undid the ribbon in his hair, shaking his head. His hair fell around his shoulders as it often did, thick and silky and with a gentle wave toward the end of it.

"I'm not criticising you, I just think it must be uncomfortable, that's all. My mother taught me to take very good care of my hair," said Thwaites, reaching around and pulling it so that it fell over one of his shoulders instead of both, and Jack looked at the ink on his neck, and the dappled scars there too from one violent encounter or another.

"*My* mother died when I was four," said Jack in a low voice. "She was very ill all my life – complications from my birth."

"You don't remember her?" asked Thwaites, looking out over the horizon and the shining blue of the ocean swells.

"Not as I remember other things," said Jack, although he had no real idea why he was answering, why he felt so compelled to answer. Thwaites beside him was warm and seemed tremendously solid, and Jack was torn between wanting to stand here beside him forever and to pull away from him. "I remember… the scent she wore, a French scent, the texture of the dresses she wore. I don't remember her face, but my father did commission a small portrait."

Thwaites chuckled, and Jack glanced at him.

"What?"

"He thinks you're poor, that's all," said Thwaites, his lips twitching in amusement. "Most of the men have assumed the same, that you're just a run of the mill lad who signed on from the docks in Bristol. Your father is Admiral John Edward Wicks, isn't he?"

Jack pressed his lips together, and then nodded.

"Money isn't everything," said Thwaites quietly. "It doesn't change how people think of us, the assumptions that are made of us."

"All of my father's wealth is in property," said Jack. "Perhaps I'd agree with you if I had any share of my father's money and didn't have to make my own way."

"Want me to have a friend kill him, get you your inheritance as soon as possible?" asked Thwaites, and Jack gave him a horrified look, but Thwaites was laughing – what sort of man joked about that? Well. The sort of man that had killed his *own* father, Jack supposed.

"You know what Poole was telling me last night?" asked Jack, feeling the urge to tell him about it suddenly burst in his chest, and Thwaites arched his eyebrows.

"Go on."

"His father is a member of the abolitionist movement," said Jack, and Thwaites started laughing, putting one of his beautiful hands over his mouth.

"Oh, bless his stupid little heart," he murmured. "He just brought that up unprompted?"

"Not exactly. But he thinks— he really does think it's about money, you know, or luck. That just because a few people say something *ought* be one way, it is that way. He's… He has no *idea* what he has at his fingertips. His wealth, the family he comes from, the influence he could so easily command, and he throws it all away to whore himself out to every passing man, never so much as makes an attempt to control himself."

"Control isn't innate for all of us," said Thwaites, giving a slight shrug of his shoulders. "I've gotten better, the older I get, but I can be…" He huffed out a small, self-deprecating sound. "Suffice it to say, it's taken me quite some years to get my temper in order, and Paul still has to pull me back from the edge at times. I see a lot of myself in him."

Jack looked down at Poole, who was laughing his pretty little head off as Creed reached out and adjusted his posture, kept moving his elbows, his waist, tipping up his chin. Poole did a plié, and then laughed when Creed said something else, and then the two of them were wrestling.

Jack raised himself up on his feet, ready to go intervene – Creed was twice Poole's size easily, and could easily do him harm just by accident – but then Poole did something that Jack couldn't quite follow with his eyes, and threw Creed bodily onto the ground. Creed landed hard on his back with a shout of surprise more than pain, and Poole looked down at him.

Jack stared, his mouth open, and heard Poole's cry of, "Oh, I'm sorry, Julius!" and "Are you alright?" as he rushed to help him up, but Creed was laughing so hard from his place sprawled on the sand that he couldn't concentrate enough for Poole to pull him to his feet.

"Quite the mystery, isn't he?" asked Thwaites in mild tones. "Sweet little thing isn't violent by nature, but he knows how to defend himself."

"Creed is a giant compared to him," said Jack softly.

"Oh, it's all about using a man's weight against him, tipping him off his balance," said Thwaites. "It's really all the more impressive that he can do it with Creed – he's got an impeccable sense of balance, what with all the covert observation of the ballet he used to do when he was still in New Orleans."

"I can't cope with him," said Jack quietly. "I know he isn't as delicate as he looks, but he's impossible to speak to about anything – ignorant of the world as he is, so entirely naïve, so certain that everyone must have it as easy as he does."

"You think he has it easy?"

"If I were embroiled in half of what he seems to have been, I'd have been hanged a dozen times over."

"You're quite right, of course," said Thwaites mildly, "had he skin like yours or mine, he'd never have been such mercy from any justice – but he does suffer things you don't. I would point out that for all your struggles, Lieutenant, people have actually made attempts on his life half a dozen times. Can the same be said of you?"

"What are you *talking* about? Who'd make an attempt on his life?"

Thwaites laughed, and patted his shoulder. "Oh, the both of you do make me laugh," he said amusedly, drawing away from him and starting to make his way back down the steps. "I don't know that there are two men the world over quite so stupid as you two. He talks, you don't listen, you mutter a few words, he can't read between the lines, you get angry that he can't divine the parts you were too cowardly to say – and then instead of asking you about it, he runs off to sulk in my lap."

Jack had no idea whatsoever what to make of that, and he came to follow after Thwaites down to the bottom of the hill.

Poole was talking in a rapid language that wasn't French or Spanish with a few of the other sailors, and judging by Creed's blank expression as he looked between them, he couldn't follow it any more than Jack could.

Poole seemed upset, had his hands clenched at his sides and was stamping his foot, which only made the sailors laugh harder, and then Poole said something so sharp that all three of them went quiet, staring at him.

One of them said something else, and all three of them laughed – and Poole's eyes flooded with tears.

Thwaites broke into this conversation now, saying something smooth and idle and easy, and when Poole opened his mouth, Thwaites grabbed him by the hair and pulled him closer, wrapping one arm around Poole's shoulder.

"These delightful men, Poole, are rather jealous of your skill, I'm afraid," said Thwaites softly. "Were any of them able to dance as you and Creed do, perhaps they wouldn't be quite so unpopular with the ladies when we make port."

Poole, teary-eyed and so red in the face he looked ready to explode, said something loud, and one of the sailors lunged for him – before Thwaites could grab him, Poole had kneed him in the crotch, and he went down to his knees with a sharp sound of pain, although Thwaites hauled him back before he could do any more damage.

"I'll deal with you three later," Thwaites barked, and Jack followed after them as Thwaites pulled Poole aside to sit, and Poole dropped down onto the chair that was beside Cotton's workbench as he carved a piece of driftwood with a face.

"Alright, lad?"

"No," said Poole. "I'm basically a girl, and I cry like one, and dance like one, and I'm a sodomite."

"None of that's new," said Cotton. "Best own up to what you are, lad, and just be better at being you than they are at being them."

Poole, wide-eyed and wet-cheeked and sniffling, stared up at him.

"Or just stop *crying*," said Jack. "Is that what they were saying to you, that you look like a girl? Do you think it helps to burst into tears?"

"You think I cry like I do on *purpose*?" demanded Poole.

"Do you see me cry over every insult bandied in my direction?"

"No, but I never see you smile, either," said Poole scowlingly. "You've all the emotional range of the Mechanical Turk, except I expect you're as easy to flounce at chess as you are at cards."

"And if you weren't so deficient you could do a thing other than play chess, cards, and doctor, perhaps they might have cause to call you something other than a sodomite or a girl."

“Mr Cotton is right,” said Poole wetly. “At least I know I’m a sodomite and good at it – you don’t have the slightest idea *what* you are.”

“You struggle to understand my identity because it doesn’t revolve around cock, Poole,” said Jack. “That’s not the same as me not knowing *what* I am.” There was more scorn on *what* than he intended, and Poole stared up at him, his lips parted, his eyes still wide. “You’re just too stupid to—”

“*Fuck* you,” hissed Poole, and stood to his feet, his fists clenched tight at his sides, his lips curled in a snarl, and a part of Jack thrilled to see him like this, so angry he wasn’t crying any longer, even though just as much of him was genuinely a little intimidated despite himself. “You think I’m stupid? Why? Because I think other people can and should be halfway decent? Because it upsets me when people call me a whoreish little bitch, whether they do it in Hungarian or some other tongue?”

“Is that what it was? Hungarian?” Jack asked, and Poole stared up at him. “Where did you learn to speak Hungarian?”

“Do you speak any language other than English?” demanded Poole.

“French and German.”

Poole spoke so rapidly that it was all a blur of noise, and although after a few seconds Jack knew that it was French, knew enough that Poole had called him *vous* instead of *tu*, called him cher, he couldn’t pick out any of the other words; when Poole followed it up with a volley in German, still using a formal pronoun, Jack set his jaw.

“Don’t be so superior, Poole,” said Thwaites. “I expect Lieutenant Wicks reads very well – not everyone has the opportunity for practice as you’ve had.”

“What, no catty comment about how I can’t read?” demanded Poole when Jack said nothing, and Jack pressed his lips hard together.

"Make up your mind," he said coolly. "Do you *want* me to be cruel to you, or not?"

"I just want you to think I'm worth something," said Poole dully, and somehow it was worse now that he wasn't crying. "You keep saying I'm a stupid useless whore even though I'm good at all sorts of things and I'll give everything a try, because coincidentally anything I happen to be good at is something you don't think is worth being good at."

"Everything I say and do, *coincidentally*, is about you," Jack retorted.

"If it's not about me, why do you have to fucking *look* at me like you do?"

"I'm not always looking at you!" snapped Jack, "sometimes I'm just fucking *looking*!" He'd raised his voice, something he always tried not to do, because he knew how uncontrolled it made him look, how people found it "intimidating" no matter how justified his anger was or who shouted at him first.

He regretted it, inwardly cringed, almost wanted to apologise even as he did it because he could just envision Poole cringing away from him – but when he looked, Poole hadn't even *flinched.*

"Just *say* that then," said Poole. "I don't fucking know the difference, do I?"

"You don't know the difference between—" Poole's eyes were flaring with heat, and Jack snapped his jaw shut. "Fine," he said. "Fine. There's nothing *wrong* with you being a sodomite – I've not the slightest problem with the men you fuck or the men that fuck you. If I'd understood what the Hungarians were saying, perhaps I'd have intervened myself. Do you *want* me to go punch their lights out?"

"Yes, please," said Poole immediately.

"*No*," said Thwaites.

"I wasn't going to do it!" said Jack.

"I didn't want him to," said Poole, his lips shifted into a small smile.

Thwaites and Cotton shared a knowing look, which Jack resented.

"Remember what I said, lad, about just telling him what you mean?" asked Cotton.

"Oh, I prefer that," said Poole. "When people just say things instead of faffing about with… with *implications*."

"That's because you can't follow implications," said Jack.

"Yes!" said Poole, stamping his foot on the ground and putting his hands on his hips. "You *know* that."

Jack stared down at him, putting his lips together. Poole wasn't as fragile as he looked, Jack knew, even like this, pale and teary-eyed and overwhelmed, and yet—

And yet.

Of the two of them, it really wasn't Poole who was the stupid one, because Jack felt *raw* with a sort of agonising want – but of course, what he didn't want was to be Poole's kept fucking man, isolated on an olive grove with him and dependent on his mercies and his charity. It would be different, if he had his own money, but he didn't, and *wouldn't*.

Poole wiped his eyes.

"Hey," said one of the Hungarians. Creed's hand was on his shoulder, and he looked nervous.

"Attila," said Poole, and then raised himself to his feet, shifted his shoulders, and smiled. He said something that Jack couldn't understand, but it was flirtatious judging by the way that Attila's mouth dropped open.

Attila said something, slightly harsh, seeming more flustered than angry – Poole replied with a sort of delicacy and a shrug of his shoulders, his voice almost a purr that sent heat flooding between Jack's legs.

"You serious?" asked Attila.

"Why?" asked Poole. "Scared to give it a try?"

Creed had taken his hand off of Attila's shoulder, making a face, and Poole smiled at all of them before he went to keep pace with him, sliding his hand around Attila's arm.

"Well," said Thwaites, smirking. "One can't say the lad isn't a master of resolving conflict."

"What, with his arse?" demanded Jack.

"If you understood Hungarian, lad, you'd know it was his mouth," said Cotton.

"Do you think you're helping?"

"No, but then, I'm not trying to help. I'm just enjoying myself, me."

Jack looked at Creed. "Did you expect this?"

"No," said Creed, and then laughed. "I never know what to expect with him. He's a bit like you that way, Captain."

"You're very sweet, Creed," said Thwaites.

"You're not going to do anything?" Jack asked.

"What do you want me to do, Wicks? Ask if we can watch?"

"I expect he'd let you," said Cotton, and Jack rolled his eyes and came to stand at his workbench with him.

* * *

It was a small island with a wide beach and cabins hidden up amidst the trees, and for two weeks as the date they'd set for the exchange approached, Gerald slept on top of Wicks. It was often on beds laid out under the trees, so that they could see the stars – the air was warm and humid, and remarkably heavy on the skin.

Thwaites showed him a cicada, held it delicately as it wriggled in his palm and beat its wings, and he pointed out to Gerald the segmentation of its body, the stained-glass appearance of its wings, the different pieces of its legs and the way they were separated and the shape of its feet, and its black beady eyes.

They were so much louder, the cicadas singing all together, than Gerald could ever have thought.

He touched himself one night when it seemed every soul on the island was asleep, muffled his gasps into his own shoulder, and Wicks reached out and grasped his wrist.

"*Wicks*," Gerald whispered harshly, feeling drawn tight as a bowstring, so close he could taste it.

"Not next to me," Wicks complained. "I can't sleep. Didn't Atilla give you what you wanted?"

"No, I just sucked him off!"

"Well, you should have negotiated better terms. Let me *sleep*."

Gerald let out a growl of fervent frustration and rolled over to go back to sleep, his cock pinned beneath him.

"Just because you're made of *stone*," he mumbled into the bed.

"I'm not," said Wicks, surprisingly soulfully. "Or I'd be able to sleep through it."

"Then—"

"*No*, Poole," said Wicks, almost desperately. "I can't… *be* the way you are."

Gerald swallowed hard, and did his best to go back to sleep.

The captain had set a two-week window.

The first day passed by and Gerald felt unwell.

The first week passed, and he *was* unwell – Wicks rubbed his back after he'd finished emptying his stomach.

"Will you kill us?" he asked Thwaites on the thirteenth day. "You mustn't kill Mr Wicks. He's only ever been a good sailor and in any case he was good on this ship too and even if he couldn't join your crew there's no reason you shouldn't just drop him off somewhere."

"Poole," said Thwaites, "do you see this book in my lap? Do you think I am holding it for decoration?"

"I don't care if you kill me," said Gerald, "but it wouldn't be preux to kill Wicks, Captain, just for the crime of being next to me – and he's, he's already had so many struggles *apart* from me, you know, being in the navy and being ill-treated just for his not being a white man, and wouldn't it be awful of you, really, to cut his life short after all that? Wouldn't that make you just as bad as the navy men who've mistreated you, when Wicks has never done a thing wrong in all his life, and been overlooked and poorly treated at every other turn?"

Thwaites stared at him a few moments, and then said, gesturing with the book, "I am reading it, in fact."

Gerald groaned, and walked away.

Wicks was sitting on a bench, braiding twine into a thicker rope. His hands, which were big and not incredibly delicate, struggled a little with the work, but he rallied to the task and kept moving anyway, such that the rope ended up good and strong anyway.

"Did Julius do your hair like that?" asked Gerald, and Wicks gave him a sidelong glance as Gerald dropped onto the bench – or, more accurately, the old log – beside him, straddling it and dropping his face against Wicks' shoulder, looking up at his hair. It looked nice like this, no longer thickly pressed down to his scalp with the pomade oil – they'd washed it out, and Wicks' hair was done in neat little twists now, so that you could see the beautiful thickness of his curling hair, all its natural bounce and life.

"*Mr Creed*," said Wicks firmly, "helped me with my hair, yes."

"He's good at everything," said Gerald quietly. "I wish I could be good at half the things he's good at. Do you think you'll grow yours out like his?"

"No, I don't think so."

"Why not? His hair's beautiful, don't you think? I can't grow my hair very long at all – it gets to about this length and then just stops, really, and grows all messy and drab." Gerald reached up, running a hand through his hair. "Of course, I've had bits of it pulled out enough, with one thing or another – I expect it thinks it knows better than to grow any longer at this point. You know, keep itself out of danger."

Wicks was giving him one of his funny looks, and Gerald put his hand back down, resting his cheek on his upper arm again.

"I have to pomade my hair in the navy," said Wicks quietly, so quietly Gerald really did have to strain to hear it, "because I have bad hair."

"But your hair is—"

"I know what my hair is," Wicks interrupted him, and Gerald closed his mouth. "They *call* it bad hair – they mean that it's not like your hair. That it's not thin and flat and straight: it's too thick, too curly, too much like wool. The only way I can get away with it *not* being called a rat's nest is to pomade it, and wear my cap as much as I can."

"Oh," said Gerald. "There's nothing you can do about that, I suppose."

"No, Poole."

"And they'd never let you have it like this, or in long dreadlocks like Julius." When Wicks gave him a look, he corrected, "Like Mr Creed."

"No."

"Would you like it like his, if you could?"

Wicks opened his mouth, closed it. Said, "I don't know that there's much point in thinking about the *coulds*, Poole, when I can't."

"Same as how you can't be with men, no matter that you'd like to," said Gerald.

"I suppose," said Wicks after a moment, and Gerald leaned into his shoulder for the last time, and stayed there now.

"I'm sorry," he said. He wanted to say more, to really say something that would make Wicks *feel* better, to comfort him, but he didn't know the first fucking thing about the navy, let alone navigating it in such a way as to get people to be less cold, less awful, and he knew by now that trying to comfort Wicks more than often just ended up making him more upset.

"… Me too," said Wicks, finally, and kept braiding his twine.

* * *

On the next day – the fourteenth day of the window Thwaites had set – white sails showed on the horizon.

Gerald felt a burst of impossible relief followed by a sudden, crushing emptiness.

They all dressed up to go down to the beach – the vessel itself anchored some ways off the shore, and coming ashore in a rowboat was not some agent of Gerald's aunt's that he'd never seen before, but to his delight and surprise, his elder brother, Percival.

"Good *Lord*, Gerry, look at you," said Percy as came to meet them, cupping his cheeks and pushing his head back to examine him. "You've skin like leather!"

"It's from the sun," said Gerald helpfully.

"Your poor hands, look at these callouses!"

"From rope, mostly."

"You've put on weight," said Percy, wavering between approval and concern.

"It's muscle."

"All these years, and I've never seen you in such an extreme condition whilst still being so… intact."

Gerald frowned up at him. "What's *that* supposed to mean?"

Percy inhaled, and he looked from Gerald to Thwaites and Cotton and Wicks, and then back down at him. "Gerry, not that I'd ever doubt you," he said, fixing Gerald's collar although Wicks had fixed it quite firmly in place, "but this *is* an actual kidnapping, and not some sort of strange sex game you're playing with these men, isn't it?"

"Oh, good," said Thwaites. "I see you know Mr Poole's proclivities quite well."

"You've hearing like a bat," snapped Gerald, turning about to look at him, to which Thwaites shrugged his shoulders. "Percival, this is Captain Thwaites and his quartermaster, Mr Cotton – dastardly pirates, they are, and my captors. And *this* is Second Lieutenant Wicks, who came with me. Captain Thwaites, this is my brother."

"Hullo, chaps," said Percy thinly. "Gerry, I have rather a lot of money back on that ship. Am I giving it to these men or not?"

"Uh," said Gerald, rather taken aback by the phrasing of the question and still rather frustrated by the implication about his proclivities, and he looked to Thwaites and Cotton.

"Don't look at me," said the latter.

"I really don't know," said Thwaites, shrugging his perfect shoulders, his lips curved into an easy smirk. "Is he going to, Poole, or isn't he?"

"Forgive me for saying so," said Percy, "but you really don't seem to have captured my brother very well. He's not even bound."

"He's here, isn't he?" asked Cotton.

"It's a great deal of effort keeping him contained," agreed Thwaites. "Easier to put him to work and walk away from him, I find, than to try some other method – we would have tied him up, but he fidgets terribly, and always finds his way out of his binds."

"Why are you— For God's sake, am I your hostage or not?" demanded Gerald.

"Well, I suppose if you go with him and we take your ransom, you are and were our hostage," said Thwaites, glancing at his fingernails. "If you don't, I expect we'd have to call you something else."

"No column marked hostage on the company roster," agreed Cotton.

"You mean… You mean I can stay?" asked Gerald.

"If you like," said Thwaites, all casual. "But I thought you wanted to pick olives."

"They *did* kidnap you in all honesty at first, didn't they?" asked Percy sharply, sounding really quite angry.

"Yes," said Gerald defensively.

"You *did* fear for your life?"

"Of course!"

"And you charmed them into wanting to keep you," said Percy flatly.

"Well, I don't think I did anything particularly—"

"This is the fucking highwaymen all over again," said Percy.

"That was years ago!"

"It was last year, Gerry, and they still send you letters!"

Gerald blustered, glancing at the pirates and Wicks, who were all looking at him with variations of horror (mostly Wicks), delight (mostly Thwaites), and irritation (mostly Cotton) writ on their faces.

"Did you bring them with you?" asked Gerald quietly, and Percy let out an irritable noise.

"You want to be a pirate now?" he demanded.

"Do you think Daddy will be angry?"

"I think he's given up with anger," said Percy. "I suppose it's better to be a pirate than a highwayman or a dancer or a gymnast or any of all that – but he *would* be angry if you got yourself killed, so… don't."

"Percy, I'd never!"

"And you should still write."

"I'd not stop just for piracy."

"Do you want money?"

"Well," said Gerald, "well, they've gone to an awful lot of trouble, Percy. How much did Daddy give you for Diane's dowry?"

Percy looked at him very flatly. "I'm not giving you that much, Gerry."

Gerald shifted slightly on his feet, and then said, in a slower, more subtle voice, "How much did he give Ben for Flora?"

Percy cleared his throat, his lips twitching as he tried not to laugh. "Well," he said. "I suppose I can give you more than that."

"Is this ship ours?"

"It's John Welch's."

"Oh, he's a terrible bore, Percy."

"I didn't call on him for his scintillation conversation, Ger, I called on him because I thought you were actually in grave danger."

"Would he give my friend Wicks a job?" asked Gerald, and Percy glanced to Wicks, who had been standing straight, hands behind his back, the whole time. "Or would you? He's quite the hero, Percy, and has been defending my honour and my virtue—"

Virtue? repeated Percy silently, looking sceptical, and Gerald shoved him in the chest.

"— and trying to keep me *safe*, all this time, even though he thinks me really quite annoying."

"Everyone thinks you annoying, Gerry," said Percy, "but of course, Second Lieutenant, I'd be glad to introduce you to Mr Welch or write you a letter of recommendation anywhere you like, if you tire of your naval commission. Any man who can handle our Gerald can handle anything the sea would give him."

"It isn't necessary, sir," said Wicks. "But thanks for thinking of me."

"He calls you sir?" asked Percy from the side of his mouth.

"I was calling *you* sir, Mr Poole," said Wicks. "I call him an irritation.

Gerald put two fingers up at him. "Virgin!"

"Whore."

Percy looked powerlessly between the two of them, and Thwaites said, "And can you believe, Mr Poole, observing this exchange, that we'd *ever* want to give them back?"

"You're made of stern stuff, Captain Thwaites," said Percy, and then patted Gerald's chest. "Gerry, how many of these men are snared in your trap?

"Two," said Thwaites.

"*One*," corrected Wicks, giving him a glare.

"Percy," said Gerald, as if butter wouldn't melt. "I only set traps for rabbits."

"I should have known it would be something like this," muttered Percy. "You don't half give me heart troubles, Gerry – I thought it would be like that mob in Ludlow again and you'd really be quite hurt."

"Oh, Captain Thwaites is nothing like all that," said Gerald.

"I'll sort out the exchange," said Percy, stepping back. "I'll be forty minutes – write a letter for Daddy explaining yourself."

Gerald hesitated.

"Write a letter," Percy corrected himself, "saying hello and that you love him and that you're *very* sorry for all the distress, and tell him it'll be the last time."

"Oh," said Gerald. "Yes, I'll do all that. Should I try to mean the last part?"

"Why bother? You've never meant it before," said Percy.

As he got back into the small boat again, where the sailors who'd accompanied him looked several shades of baffled, Gerald turned to Cotton, Thwaites, and Wicks, who were wearing similar expressions to the ones they had before.

"Can I kill him now, Ced?" asked Cotton.

"I begin to think, Paul," said Thwaites pleasantly, taking a puff of his cigarillo, "that you couldn't manage it if you tried."

Gerald shifted on his feet. "He's really blowing the thing about the highwaymen quite out of proportion. They only took me, you see, because I'd been travelling with this caravan who'd picked me up after I offended this Austrian fellow, and then I left to be with the circus for a bit, juggling and doing card tricks, you know, but the highwaymen actually thought when they kidnapped me that I was—"

Wicks was coming closer, moving across the sand, and Gerald trailed off, looking up at him.

"How many times have you been kidnapped?" asked Wicks.

"Oh, quite a few times," said Gerald softly. "I believe I have mentioned it, once or twice – you could almost call it a hobby."

"And those… And people have tried to kill you," said Wicks.

"Oh, yes, lots of times," said Gerald, smiling. "I've told Captain Thwaites all about a few of the times, and Ju— Mr Creed. It's really no secret."

"You've never told me."

"Well, you'd get angry over stories like that," said Gerald. "I'm never allowed to tell them at dinner – they're not for polite company, my father says, and you're just about the politest company I've ever had. Are you— Are you really not going to go with him?"

"No," said Wicks solidly, his expression unreasonably. "Seems to me I've duties still here. With you. If you're to… I can hardly let you join a pirate crew on your own, with you being the way you are. You need *some* sort of chaperone."

"Oh," said Gerald, and suddenly he was smiling so wide he thought his face might split. "Yes. I— I've always rather wanted a chaperone."

"We'll have to split the dowry," said Thwaites.

"We will do no such thing," said Wicks, and lifted Gerald up by the hips to kiss him.

Gerald gasped and kissed him back, wrapped his legs around Wicks' waist and marvelled at his strength, felt dizzy and wonderful and as if he might burst. "What about God?" he asked breathlessly against his mouth.

"God can be bargained with," said Wicks. "I suppose we'll just have to get married."

Gerald's cheeks burned. "Oh," he said. "Oh, I've never been *married* before."

"What a nice thing to set marriage apart from everything else."

"Jack, will you be this horrible and sharp and cutting with me for all our lives?" asked Gerald, almost on the verge of excited tears as he asked, and Wicks laughed breathlessly, and it was really the most wonderful sound Gerald had ever heard.

"For the time being," said Wicks. "Rest assured, I will do my best to hone the blade with time."

Gerald giggled, and kissed him again.

When Wicks released him, putting him down on the sand, Thwaites asked, "Is he very good at kissing, Poole?"

"No, sir," said Gerald. "He's quite terrible."

"*Gerald,*" complained Wicks. "I am no such thing."

"May I try?" asked Thwaites. His hands were loosely held behind his back – Cotton was now smoking his cigarillo, and sipping heavily from a pocket flask – and he was looking at Wicks very keenly, all the beautiful constellations in his eyes shining in the light.

Wicks stared at him. "A marriage, I might remind you, is between two people," he said.

"I've not the least interest in marrying either of you," said Thwaites, "although some marriages certainly allow for more than two parties. What I'd like very much for now, Wicks, is to kiss you. What's more, I think you'd like for me to kiss you too."

"And fuck Gerald with me too, I suppose?"

"Or fuck you with him," said Thwaites. "Variety *is* the spice of life, I'm told."

"Lad," said Cotton, "if you really don't want to, you don't *ha*—"

Wicks dipped Thwaites to kiss him as though the two of them were dancers, and it sent Thwaites' hat falling to the hand, one of his hands coming up to cup Wicks' cheek.

Gerald felt hot all over.

"There," said Wicks, keeping Thwaites tilted backward as their mouths broke apart. "Do you think I'm bad?"

"Young man," said Thwaites kindly, "you've more than enough time to practise."

Giggling, Gerald managed to catch him before Wicks could drop him on the sand.

"I'm still not splitting the dowry," said Wicks to Cotton as Gerald and Thwaites began to kiss again, and this time, no one stopped Gerald from undoing Thwaites' belt.

"If it's any consolation, Jack," said Cotton, offering him the flask, "I don't think it's the dowry he's interested in splitting."

FIN.

From the Author

Hello!

My name is Johannes T. Evans, and I hope you've enjoyed this novella, *Gerald Poole and the Pirates*. If you have, I'd very much appreciate you leaving a positive review on whatever review site is your favourite!

If you'd like to seek out more of my work, *Heart of Stone* is a full-length novel also set in the 18th century, and is a slowburn slice-of-life romance between a vampire and his secretary.

If you're interested in perusing more novella-length pieces and short stories, I publish a huge variety of short stories that are available on a subscription model from Patreon or as part of your Medium subscription! My name is Johannes T. Evans on both sites.

My website: www.JohannesTEvans.com

My TeePublic, for merchandise: @JohannesTEvans

My Twitter: @JohannesTEvans

And finally, if you'd like to get regular email updates from me, with media recommendations, links to my most recently published work, and other little announcements, you can sign up at www.buttondown.email/JohannesTEvans.

Printed in Great Britain
by Amazon

27805201R00079